The Crab Nebula

The Crab Nebula

Le Nébuleuse du crabe

Eric Chévillard

Translated by
Jordan Stump and
Eleanor Hardin

 University of Nebraska Press
Lincoln & London

*Publication of this translation was
assisted by a grant from the French
Ministry of Culture.*

© 1993 by Les Éditions de Minuit
Translation copyright © 1997 by
the University of Nebraska Press.
All rights reserved. Manufactured
in the United States of America.
⊗ The paper in this book meets
the minimum requirements of
American National Standard for
Information Sciences – Perma-
nence of Paper for Printed Libra-
ry Materials, ANSI Z39.48-1984.
Set in Font Company Vendome
& Bitstream Maritime symbols
by Tseng Information Systems.
Book design: Richard Eckersley.

Library of Congress
Cataloging in Publication Data
Chevillard, Eric.
[Nébuleuse du crabe. English]
The crab nebula = La nébuleuse
du crabe / Eric Chevillard;
Translated by Jordan Stump and
Eleanor Hardin.   p.   cm.
ISBN 0-8032-1475-8 (cl: alk. paper). –
ISBN 0-8032-6370-8 (pa: alk. paper)
I. Stump, Jordan, 1959–.
II. Hardin, Eleanor. III. Title.
PQ2663.H432N4313 1997 843'.914-dc20
96-19972 CIP

Introduction

This is not exactly the story of a man who could not quite make up his mind. Not at all, in fact: Crab's indecision was decided for him long before he could have had any say in the matter, long before he came or did not come into existence. Indecision and inconstancy make up the very fiber of his being, along with a certain penchant for the extreme. For Crab's nature—his life itself—hangs by a slender thread: language. And language, thank goodness, expresses both the impossible and the possible with the same blithe dexterity; moreover, if left to its own devices, it drifts merrily and ineluctably down a never-ending stream of associations and enumerations. It is this unstoppability and this freedom that determine the shape of Crab's experience. It would seem that if language can speak it, Crab will eventually live through it.

But Crab is no plaything. He bears his lot stoically and sometimes joyfully. With all the considerable force of his reason, he strives to mold the world around him to his liking. His success is never quite unmixed—nothing about Crab is unmixed—but we might at least admire his persistence, however risible or pathetic it may prove in the end. He will never give up trying to step into the same stream twice.

We might envy Crab on at least one point: he has found in Éric Chevillard a Boswell of astonishing diligence and perspicacity. For, just as Valéry did for Monsieur Teste, Michaux for Plume, Jarry for Docteur Faustroll, or Rabelais for Gargantua, Chevillard has chosen to offer us a subtle and detailed portrait of an extraordinary man from whose every act we ordinary folk have much to learn. And there is a wealth of acts to learn from; Chevillard has given us a full-length portrait of Crab, from the moment of his birth or lack thereof straight through to his many demises, by way of the innumerable revelations, doubts, fervors, and loose ends of his eventful childhood, his difficult relationships with women, a handful of nascent or abortive careers, his travels, his slow descent into the helplessness of old age and ever-impending death.

The moral of his story? "To thine own self be true," perhaps; Crab asks for nothing more than the chance to do just that. If only his self were a little more inclined to be true to him.

Éric Chevillard was born in 1964 in the quiet provincial town of La Roche-sur-Yon. He published his first novel, *Mourir m'enrhume,* at the age of twenty-three and went on to publish six more in short order: *Le Démarcheur* (1989), *Palafox* (1990), *Le Caoutchouc décidément* (1992), *La Nébuleuse du crabe* (1993), *Préhistoire* (1994), and *Un fantôme* (1995). In each of his works (but always from different angles) Chevillard explores two fundamental questions: How can we possibly claim to understand the world around us, and how might we reshape that world into something comprehensible and workable? With the logic of desperation, his characters struggle endlessly to find an answer—none more valiantly than Crab, and none more (or less) successfully.

Chevillard is part of a particularly fascinating development in the French literary scene: the rise of a nonmovement centered around one of France's most distinguished and distinctive publishing houses, the Éditions de Minuit, home to Samuel Beckett and, most notably, to the *nouveau roman* of the 1950s. Since the middle of the 1980s, Minuit has gathered together a remarkable assembly of authors (Marie Redonnet, Jean Echenoz, and Eugène Savitzkaya, for instance) who, like Chevillard, are pushing the French novel in surprising new directions. And *different* directions: the only common features of these "jeunes auteurs de Minuit" are an attraction to the extremes of literary style—from the denuded to the baroque—and an uneasiness at the idea of alliance to a group or school. Little surprise, then, that while Chevillard feels the influence of Lautréamont, Beckett, Michaux—and, interestingly, the painter Jean Dubuffet —he cannot consider them his masters or mentors; as he says, these are precisely the sort of creators who do not want disciples. The same is undoubtedly true of Chevillard himself, and so we cannot hope, with this first English translation of his work, to attract disciples to his (or to Crab's) cause. We are sure, however, that this astonishing book will earn them both more than a few admirers.

We would like to thank those whose kind assistance made this translation possible: Tom Vosteen, Warren Motte, and most particularly Éric Chevillard.

Jordan Stump / Eleanor Hardin

The Crab Nebula

Given a choice between deafness and blindness, Crab would lose his hearing on the spot, without a moment's hesitation. Yet he values music far more than painting. And this is not Crab's only contradiction, as we shall see. If he then had to choose between his right eye and his right hand, he would sacrifice his right eye. Similarly, if he were forced to decide between his left eye and his left hand, he would opt for the latter. He would sooner keep his left hand than his right eye, and he would preserve his right hand at the expense of his left eye. But ask him to choose between both eyes and both hands, he who claimed to prefer either of his hands to either of his eyes, and he will gladly give up both hands in order to retain both eyes.

We should expect nothing more from Crab. There is no point in urging him to prove less erratic or more logical in his choices. Crab is ungraspable, not evasive or deceptive but blurry, as if his congenital myopia had little by little clouded his contours.

A live garter snake serves as a sheath for his sword. He never utters a thought that he does not, a few moments later, refute with all his might and on the strength of overwhelming evidence, only to attack that selfsame evidence with devastating reasoning, discrediting it once and for all, unless of course some further information should come to light. And Crab is always prepared to supply that further information. His course of conduct is never easy to follow.

And then, Crab is not one of those people who say, "You can't compare this to that." He fails to see what could prevent him from comparing, for example, a dog to a needle. On the contrary, nothing could be simpler than to point out their differences, their respective virtues, their unique properties, their specifications—size, weight, volume, etc.—which he then need only juxtapose and contrast, enabling him to hand down an authoritative judgment in favor of the dog or the needle, the sun or the ashtray, hate or the orange, the countryside or the umbrella, exile or reading, a certain philosopher or lead. And for the incredulous, he begins his demonstration again, point by point, patiently, varying his vocabulary.

But be aware that Crab never bases his decision on a given object's purely utilitarian superiority over another. He cares nothing for such petty concerns. If he has concluded that on the whole the dog outstrips the needle, that the dog is globally superior to the needle, and if he must then sew on a missing button, Crab uses the dog. A passerby, watching him struggle at his task, will inevitably point out to him that he would have long since finished the job if he had used a needle. And Crab will have to loose his dog on him, to prove to this genius that he had reasoned rightly, and even forcefully.

This is only the beginning, but already Crab shows himself to his best advantage. It would seem that, for once, we are not dealing with just anyone. This is only a first impression; it remains to be confirmed.

There was one decisive day in Crab's life, an obligatory reference: a morning when everything seemed alien to him. Looking in the mirror, on reflection, he realized that he himself was the anomaly. He gazed at his razor on the glass shelf, his toothbrush, his comb: what is it all for? And those shoes ready to set off, one toward the orient, one toward the occident, those clothes piled on a chair, what did they expect from him—what deportment, what resolve, what solemn gestures? And what vigor, already deserting him—before he has even dressed—just to stand upright? Crab had let himself fall back onto his bed. Suddenly he no longer understood what he was about, what he was doing there, and especially what he was supposed to do in order not to disappoint, in order to perform his function, what function, and how to proceed, and where to begin, to begin what?

Perhaps he would find the answer to his questions outside, out in the real world. He would have to go and see. Crab finally decided to leave the house, but, unable to recall whether it was the two feet or the two hands that were to be employed for walking, he hesitated a moment, then opted for the hands, wider and better articulated than the feet, and somewhat flatter; besides, it seemed imprudent to put too much distance between the ground and his head, whose four senses, ever vigilant, would show him the way, helping him to avoid all manner of obstacles, for this, curiously, he remembered: that there would be obstacles, bushes, ditches, milestones, puddles, needles, anthropomorphic (so to speak) dog-droppings (for, having so long eaten from their masters' plates and shared in their endeavors, dogs have already learned to

3

produce admirable simulacra of human turds, very life-like reproductions, and the rest will follow—proof positive of the unequalled pedagogical efficacy of example and imitation). But that morning, an example was precisely what Crab did not have before him—how does a man behave? He was forced to rely on intuition alone. Hands or feet: in the end, he had an even chance of hitting on the right one, given that the unequal length of arms and legs prohibits both the active participation of all four members and the more modest cooperation of one arm and one leg; indeed, the limited scope of their articulations prevents even so much as a single step in the latter position.

Crab had opted for the hands, and when, on the street, having traveled a hundred meters or so without difficulty, he came across his fellow men, their demeanor showed him his mistake. He did as they did: proudly held his head up and fell to his knees. One shoulder for the yoke, one shoulder for the cross—but Crab shook himself free. The eccentricity was not his. It was the others who were in the wrong. What he had hastily conceded to be a blunder was, quite the contrary, a masterly setting-to-rights enabled by the failure of his memory and the confusion of his mind that morning. Leaving the house, Crab had instinctively used the means of locomotion proper to men, forgotten after some misstep or earthquake threw mankind to its feet, an abnormal stance maintained by force of habit against the dictates of common sense, and which the human race—unable to conceive of a better alternative, or any alternative at all—perpetuated from generation to generation, but without ever really attaining equilibrium or happiness — even today, they still long for that original order, believing it to be lost forever (when in fact it is only reversed), and remain dimly aware, perhaps, of their error, witness the envious admiration granted to acrobats who dance on their hands; thus Crab continued on his way amid applause.

3 No one and nothing will dissuade him—your saliva would be better used to water your garden—he will not reconsider his decision. Crab has chosen madness. Rest assured that this is no sudden brainstorm. Brainstorms are just so much wind. This is a long-cherished project, well ripened. After years of reflection and daily exercise of his intelligence, Crab has discovered that madness is indeed his only real defense against both mediocrity and boredom (which live together). He will not restate here the rigorous reasoning that led to this discovery; that would in itself conflict with his newfound principles. Suffice it to say that death lies at both ends.

How does one go mad? For it is no easy task. The mind that ponders this problem will never come up with anything but methods, and any method is in the end an attempt to order the motion of the heavens. Will Crab have to invest in a trepan? other tools? tongs? a rasp? Or is it enough simply to concentrate, until he becomes so wired that he blows his intellectual fuses? So that this tough, all-too-lucid consciousness, this brilliant star—sharp, trenchant, incisive, penetrating, able to graft night onto day—might suddenly disintegrate, dispersed, diffuse, defused: the birth of a nebula.

But Crab will seek no help from alcohol, nor from psychotropic drugs. Not for him those few short hours of intoxication or unconsciousness during which everything around him keeps up its steady pace. What good does it do to simulate stupefaction in the form of that pathetic carnival mask with its glassy eyes, blotched cheeks, great violet ears, and great red swollen nose, or to hire the services of streetwalking hallucinations, fresh from some exotic herb garden or mushroom bed, forgotten the next morning but for the empty compact they leave behind? Crab's desire is to sink into madness, headfirst, head alone, to enjoy possession only of his unhinged body, to wander on long, wide, well-kept lawns, in the gracious care of men dressed in white linen, housed in an airy, impregnable room, fed on dairy products, tenderized meat, and fish without bones—and without that great staring eye that constitutes their entire head and sends chills down one's spine. On the whole, it is a modest ambition.

How to go about it, then? Crab's efforts invariably turn against him. Diligence and perseverance—necessary if he is to avoid slacking off on his resolution of absolute indifference and reacting despite himself to every little stimulus presented by the outside world, if he is to remain permanently in that dazed condition he seeks to maintain at the price of eternal vigilance—diligence and perseverance only stoke the fires of Crab's anxiety, fostering nervous tension, an irritable perfectionism, the desire to order the world according to his own laws, soothing for himself, merciless for others.

Crab envied the brutishness of animals, their purely organic life (without the horror of organs), their purely sensual life (without the terror of the senses), their freedom from worry; he aspired to the slovenly, dreamy madness of the flabbiest octopus, the flattest lizard, the sleepiest caterpillar. But what stalks him now is a maniacal madness, devoid of comfort: niggling, cautious, meticulous, a frenzy for order and symmetry—not an immense park in which to wander, unkempt, eyes rolling, hands hanging limp, but a geometric hell as clean and cold as the depths of winter, run by a school of allergists, and Crab in the middle of it all, impeccably dressed, and the door noiselessly closing.

Every butterfly carries on its wings the precise dose of fairy dust required to make Crab believe, for one brief moment, that the world is as he likes it. But as the effects of the hallucinogen fade, he once again finds himself anxious, melancholy; his cold delirium drags him through apocalyptic landscapes deserted even by the birds—it seems to him the trees are losing their leaves, the days are growing shorter, that sort of thing, aberrations, and the wind bites at his bones.

(What Crab wants then is a nice bowl of soup in which to soak his frozen feet.)

Crab could very well have done without his wax tongue. How are you supposed to live with a wax tongue? He has to pay strict attention to what he eats. No hot drinks for Crab, no herb teas, no coffee. And yet the question of nourishment is not the most troubling—no sizzling meats either, of course, no casseroles, only simple food served cold (vegetables, fruits), preferably of creamy or pasty consistency (soft cheeses, flans), but nevertheless Crab manages to feed himself—no, his principal concern is the ineluctable stiffening of his tongue. In order to slow the process, Crab is forced to talk continuously, even if it means saying nothing of interest (and after all, how could he be expected to hold his audience spellbound twenty-four hours a day?). Inevitably, there are dull patches in his discourse, slow spots, irksome repetitions. Freed of this constraint, Crab would finally be able to contribute to a conversation only as necessary and appropriate; his words would be more highly valued; his observations—unfailingly judicious—would be known as such; his opinions would carry weight. But that would be too much to hope for; should Crab fall silent, his tongue will immediately and irreversibly solidify in his mouth. So he speaks, he says anything at all, something and its opposite, that the elephant should dress in buckskin, and he is dismissed as delirious when in fact he is fighting for his life.

Similarly, life would be easier for Crab without those mercury eyelids of his; he wouldn't look so sullen, so eternally and unappealingly morose, and his gaze, now undimmed, might reveal hidden, faraway beauties, filling him with delight. With good teeth made of ivory rather than after-dinner mints, with fingernails made of finger-nail instead of frost, with hair in place of that warm snot, with fewer scales, fewer feathers, not so much saltpeter on his belly, two feet of the same length, without that blue eye in his nostril, without those ears running along his sides, without that scrotum under his chin, without the myriad taste buds that line his intestines, life really would be much easier for Crab. A small operation would be advisable, of course, but the mere thought of it scares him out of his skin.

This morning he put on three socks from three different pairs, yet again. It's the same story every day. Because on top of everything else, Crab is the absent-minded sort.

Search a room for an object that isn't there, but search hard, mind you, and long—as long as it takes—and patiently, with a magnifying glass, with a fine-toothed comb, and you will, in the end, in spite of it all, put your finger on it. That is Crab's opinion. The demonstration follows.

5

Open your eyes wide. Look: Crab lays his pipe on the little round table in the living room. Then he walks to his bedroom, enters, and closes the door behind him. He feels like smoking a pipe. He pats his pockets, no pipe, glances at the bedside table, no pipe, the desk, no pipe—where the. . . !—he draws back the curtain covering the entrance to the bathroom: the immortal soul of a cake of soap in its saucer, the razor, the toothbrush, and the glass lined up under the hostile mirror, no pipe—what the. . . !—Crab does an about-face, sweeps the bedroom floor with his gaze, slowly, methodically, back and forth, superimposes a grid over the surface, really no pipe, not even the shadow of one, not even the smoke, not even a stem. Crab raises himself up on tiptoe, irritated, his hand blindly inspects the top of the armoire—*memento, homo, quia pulvis es*—he dusts himself off, sneezes, the trail is cold as ash, no pipe. Not under the cushion of the armchair either. Crab must recognize that he was wrong. His theory does not hold up. He openly admits it. All the same, a small doubt persists in the back of his mind. But he must bow down before the facts. And as he is humbly bowing down he triumphs, finding the pipe, at last, under the bed.

Are you convinced? Or do you want him to repeat the experiment?

Believe him or not, Crab doesn't care, here is the story: A camel assured him that he could easily pass through the eye of a needle. "What could be so difficult about that? Even water can manage it, and I can go for days without a drop." Furthermore, he was prepared to prove it, "whenever you like." Then, seeing that Crab was busy, he went on his way, adding "Give me a call when you find one in that haystack."

Crab is teaching himself to paint, but without paint for now, or brushes or canvas: that would be a waste of material. The most basic principles of painting mean nothing to Crab; he has everything to learn—the use of the laws of perspective in order to create the illusion of volume, relief, and depth to begin with, but also the technique involved in juxtaposing, opposing, and blending colors—so he practices in his head, sketching invisible shapes freehand, gesticulating furiously or minutely wriggling two fingers, depending on whether he is filling in a vast background or painstakingly adding a detail, attempting, in this preliminary phase, simply to reproduce an object present before him, seeking to develop the technique and the mastery he will need in order to undertake vast imaginary compositions that for the moment he scarcely dares dream of.

All the same, Crab is making progress; while his first attempts were amateurish (he destroyed them furiously with a flurry of violent kicks to the air), he can now manage to depict what is irrefutably a cow standing in a field that is, down to the merest blade of grass, identical to the one he sees from his window in the morning. Later in the day, the wind lifts the diaphanous muslin of the curtain, revealing the mandrill-buttocked sunset: Crab proves to be an unparalleled landscape artist, a subtle colorist—albeit without color and thus difficult to appreciate properly.

To be frank, his work could be accused of a certain academic quality; indeed, the cow is in itself academic, virtually an academician, and its very dung, academic like no other variety of shit can ever be.

But today Crab believes that he has finally mastered the art, enabling him to break through the bovine forms which contain the world, lines and circles, all that chalk geometry, to erase it, to intensify the seven colors to the point of dazzlement or to attenuate them to the point of transparency—we can soon expect great changes on the earth, under the sea, and in the heavens.

"This is a very delicate task, requiring great concentration; I need to be left alone."

So speaks the silkworm living in Crab's intestine.

Never again will people be disappointed upon opening a mussel shell; they will find a real eye, gray, blue, green, or brown. The delightful surprise one feels at the first exchange of glances will be preserved.

Because it is absurd, thinks Crab, to bury the dead with their two perfectly good (but ever so fragile) eyes, all the while taking care to remove their jewelry—stones and metals born of the earth, where they could well spend a little more time and no harm done—when we would be only too happy to give up the lot if it meant we could preserve, fully intact and everlastingly alive, the loving gaze those eyes used to favor us with.

And because it is unacceptable, continues Crab, for mussels to occupy such vast expanses without some kind of payback: they cover our coastlines like so many shiny little shoes carefully set out on the rocks by walking dolls who, unable to swim, will never return from their tragic dip in the sea, and whose lovely drifting multicolored skirts have come to be known as jellyfish. Unfortunately no. This illusion does not stand up to scrutiny. Autopsy reveals that all mussels conceal within their shells the same rubbery bonbon, that rotten bean, that dab of rancid butter, that tortoise dropping, a dubious mouthful that quickly becomes nauseating, spat out along with the lively little portunid that shares its home.

Let us praise Crab's initiative. Either of the two excellent reasons he has specified would, of course, have sufficed to convince us of its value. The eye will be quite at home in that bivalve shell, grafted onto the adductor muscle, periodically refreshed by the salty tide, winking and weeping much as ever. Relatives and friends will have only to open the precious shell to bathe once again in the limpid gaze that gave them life.

Should we, conversely, relocate the displaced mussels to the empty orbits of the cadaver? That decision will be left to the families. Crab believes that it would be indiscreet and ill advised to legislate such matters.

Is he really the only one who knows that seashells are nothing more than chintzy, quaint, mass-produced gewgaws? A merchant vessel transporting a large shipment of these knickknacks was sunk by pirates. The manufacturers went bankrupt and had no choice but to close down their factories. The matter was forgotten. Occasionally a wave throws a handful of those shells onto the beach, now inhabited by gentle, fearful mollusks—and so today it is widely and naively assumed that they are products of the sea rather than cups, brooches, whistles, and thimbles. By everyone but Crab.

Crab is the inventor of the bleak picture machine. A wonderfully ingenious and efficient machine, easily mastered after a few weeks' practice. Crab has every reason to be proud of it. Nevertheless, the National Institute of Industrial Property refuses to give him a patent, remarking that his invention is no different from an ordinary typewriter.

As a general rule, Crab's contributions to science do not arouse the interest they deserve, as for instance his invisible varnish which, when applied to a mirror, causes your reflected face to glow with pride and satisfaction, no matter your usual expression, no matter your real opinion of yourself, so that each morning you will seem pleasantly surprised to find that you are yourself.

But Crab could list one example after another.

His project for a revolutionary cosmogony—for we certainly aren't going to remain mired in the spherical forever, are we?—well, that grandiose project is given a cool reception by the scientific experts.

And why would that be, if not because those gentlemen are dying of jealousy?

Thus, the Nobel prize for physics was awarded to Professor Y. for his remarkable work on flaming disintegration, whereas Crab will have to make do yet again with the Nobel peace prize, having stolen and destroyed the plans for Professor Y.'s horrific invention.

8 Crab is endeavoring to draw the swallows, one by one, every one. Otherwise who would do it? The difficulty lies —in their number, of course, but that is only a matter of patience, of perseverance, which Crab does not lack—no, it lies more in the risk of drawing the same swallow twice. Luckily, Crab's memory is superb. He is also very conscientious. When a swallow dies, he burns the drawing that depicted it, a dated and henceforth useless document.

As we know, Crab's ambitions are modest. When he has varnished the whales, he will consider himself satisfied. When he has given to the tortoise the wings of the falcon, to the falcon the elastic legs of the frog, to the frog the finery of the peacock, to the peacock the antlers of the deer, to the deer the webbed feet of the swan, to the swan the tail of the lion, to the lion the crest of the cock, to the cock the eyes of the owl, to the owl the fins of the salmon, and to the salmon the shell of the tortoise, when he has righted these many wrongs, Crab will consider himself satisfied.

But not before.

And then it will be time to think about revarnishing the whales.

Crab is fighting for the abolition of privilege, for the pooling of those talents received at birth, and for their just and equitable redistribution. The same arms for all, the same tools from the start, the same basic material, and then all will be free to make use of them according to their desires, to develop their individual tastes and

18

distastes, to follow their own inclinations—and thus to become a bear or a mosquito or a seahorse.

And if the sparrow does not take advantage of its little built-in motor to soar with the swallows, then we can be certain that it does not mind hopping through the snow. And if the mole, endowed with an eagle eye, chooses to live on cherries and grapes, then we will know that it was only by sheer force of will that it used to choke down larvae, fighting back its disgust so as not to die of hunger. And if men, despite their forked tongues, continue to kiss women, despite their razor-like canines, then it will be confirmed that love can do without tenderness.

Crab further suggests that we now have enough fire on Earth to convert it to a sun.

9 Once again that sudden frenzy gets hold of Crab, propelling him toward the piano where once again he realizes that while the virtuosity in his fingers allows him to lift the lacquered lid of the keyboard with genuine brio, the concert abruptly ends there. Nevertheless, Crab leans over the treasure thus revealed, burning with covetousness; he reaches out and sweeps up a fistful of precious jewels, ivory and ebony, but they instantly crumble in his hand, dulled, diminished, like the emerald and the gold doubloon glittering in the water at your feet but which are transmuted into a shard of glass and a bottle cap upon contact with the corrosive sea air, too good to be true. Cast back into the water, however, they regain all their beauty; similarly, no sooner has Crab lifted his fingers from the keyboard than the wounds heal and silence miraculously returns—a wondrous thing, and all the more so when one considers that licensed healers commonly proceed, quite to the contrary, by the laying-on of hands.

But music is something Crab cannot grasp; it escapes him, it flows through his fingers, it turns hard in his mouth. His violin and clarinet improvisations were no more successful than his works for piano—the heavens open, here is the long-awaited cloudburst come to ripen the tomatoes, and Crab, having replaced the slate on his roof with xylophone bars, attracts every bolt of lightning.

Thus he has wisely resolved to abandon these traditional instruments and create new ones for his own use, better adapted to his hand, his particular gifts. He will use stone, sponge, the feet of lobsters and ostriches, hornbill beaks, sperm whale bladders, skate cartilage, whole giraffe skeletons. From these he will produce new sounds, new notes, a scale like a young eel, a rejuvenated music. Not immediately, to be sure, but as soon as he learns to play them. After all, the first organ maker could not possibly have known how to play the organ. And how could the first luthier have known how to play the lute, never in his entire life having seen or held a lute before this one, pristine, born of his own hands, a strange and beautiful object that out of inexperience he first treated as a drum, then patiently taught himself to form chords, and that he only fully mastered many long years later?

If each passerby strikes a chord on the same piano, the last one to come along will produce only strident plaints and broken phrases, no surprise there. Each must forge his own instrument, and Crab is not the first to say so. That's the conclusion of all that.

Crab was also a mediocre flutist. He was taught by the finest instructors. He wore out his ten fingers, one phalange after another (similarly, the runner who trains on an emery track ends up legless). Crab kept at it. The flute never left his mouth, his slightest sigh passed through it, remaining just as hoarse all the way through, his breath flailing and flustered from one end to the other, turning gamely back into it once it had made its way out, a little train, puffing, grinding, careening, on the wrong track from the start. His efforts were not repaid. Crab remained a mediocre flutist until the day the miracle occurred, the day it all finally fell into place: a nightingale perched upon his flute and sang.

Nevertheless, Crab has a good ear. He is not the type to confuse the heavy, imposing silence emanating from a dead elephant with the unique vibration of the air that indicates the presence of a silent bird in the surrounding greenery. And Crab could even tell you the name of the bird.

His long practice of solitary meditation has taught him, if nothing else, to distinguish the many forms of silence, which meet with only an unchanging and obtuse insensitivity in the untrained ear. There is, then—among others—a string silence, a wind silence, a percussion silence, no more alike than the instruments thus classified, but on occasion their sonorities meld into a symphonic silence in which slow, stately movements, or martial ones, alternate with sprightly little phrases and silky arabesques, playing on a variety of motifs and rhythms in order to fully express the complexity of the situation, whatever that situation may be.

(Nor does Crab forget the variety of silence derived from flour or soot.)

Judging by the particular grain of a given silence, or the uniquely crystalline nature of another, he can immediately and infallibly predict by what or by whom it will finally be broken. Gauging their weight, their density, their depth or thickness, allowing for the area and the nature of the terrain they cover, Crab calculates with astonishing precision the duration of these silences, down to the second. Thus forewarned, he can flee and take shelter elsewhere well before the noise erupts, gliding from place to place, already off again as soon as he has arrived, unable to maintain the silence and utterly powerless to impose it; indeed—just as the darkness produced by the eyelids is impotent against a lighthouse and a double row of streetlights—between wax and cotton, you might as well plug your ears with two hornets.

But a seeing-eye dog would be of great use to Crab, so weak is his sense of smell.

10 One Sunday, under the arcades of a square near his home, Crab met bliss incarnate in the form of a jazz trumpeter. To be sure, he had seen joyous expressions before, the same smile gracing two faces, four eyes shining like the four illuminated windows of a bedroom overlooking a street down which he sadly ambled. But the next couple he saw displayed only a shared moroseness: a man and a woman more advanced in age and in love than the others, but still forming only one being, like the front and back halves of a ruminant, condemned to chew endlessly the straw covering the floor of its owner-occupied prison.

There is only one way to be happy on this Earth. This was Crab's sudden revelation. One must be a jazz trumpeter.

In the current state of things, every man yearning for happiness would have to drop what he is doing and bring to his lips a trumpet, that instrument which redirects the winds of disaster and transforms the breath of a solitary soul into cheers erupting from the thousand breasts of a crowd of revelers.

That Sunday, under the arcades, Crab had thought that yes, perhaps, happiness truly might be possible for the world if only everyone would follow the example of that glorious musician, who took in through his nose the surrounding air, saturated with infections, exhaust, viruses, and dark ideas, and recirculated it cleansed of all those miasmata, as fresh as the first springtime on Earth before the blooming of the pestilential daisies, as fresh as the first bluegill before it began to stink of fish: a crisp air, vibrant, and the perspective trembled as far as the eye could see, and even the robust pillars of the arcades shivered with delight rather than shrugging their shoulders as they inevitably do when men come near.

To supply everyone with a trumpet, the distribution would certainly pose problems, but those could be overcome. Then people would have to know how to play it—the trumpet, that is—you can't just improvise, at least not before you learn to play it—where would they find the teachers? enough teachers? And even if they did find enough dedicated teachers, can you imagine six or seven billion novice trumpeters blowing into their instruments at the same time? We would see the moon in free fall, paying a return visit to Earth, and the terrified rivers leading the oceans in a retreat back to the streams.

In any case, the musician had finished his piece and laid his trumpet in the case lying open before him, after having removed the coins—also made of brass—of which a handful of hurried music lovers had relieved themselves as they passed by and which he was now counting with a glum look, a haggard face, unrecognizable, you can't play the trumpet twenty-four hours a day. Crab's initial project collapsed, but the idea that had inspired it remained valid. It would simply have to be done without trumpets.

Man himself would exhale *joie de vivre*. This would require only a few modifications to his inadequate respiratory system. And Crab began to draw up plans, a series of diagrams in cross-section showing the principal respiratory organs, filling his sheet of paper with a multitude of delicate operations, connecting and disconnecting the tracheal artery, transplanting the bronchial tubes, enlarging or compressing the lungs—and blood

25

no longer had anything to do with it, the blood of his ancestors of which Crab knows himself to be the repository and the guarantor (no less than of their evaporated urine), blood that inevitably betrays the assassin, blood that is closely followed by tears. He deviated, obstructed, blocked off canals, he simplified and perfected the respiratory apparatus, so that toxic vapors, far from damaging the system, will be treated, filtered, purified, and finally expelled, returned to the blue heavens: the headiness of the mountaintop will roll into the valley, spill into the narrow streets, the stuffy rooms, the dank basements, the revivified atmosphere will spontaneously give birth to hummingbirds.

A few little improvements like that, concludes Crab, and everything looks just a bit brighter.

When things begin to go to his head, Crab takes off his boots, no longer needed.

Call it foresight or intuition, Crab acquired at a very tender age the certainty that he was destined to play a great role in History despite his obscure birth, his pathetic intellectual abilities, his feeble physical condition, and the daily-confirmed unsightliness of his face. Thus, from childhood on, he strove to prove worthy of his glorious future.

His first task was to build a wooden pedestal, easily disassembled and transported, upon which—once he had completed a sonorous inaugural address—he would hoist himself, not without a certain emotion, in any location he deemed worthy of that honor. And he would remain there for several hours, motionless, frozen in a flattering pose.

The brilliance of his future renown thus illuminated many deserted and desolate squares, rainy intersections, promontories, city centers. Since he could not yet know what prowess, what exceptional merit would earn him (this alone was certain) universal admiration and thanks, Crab varied his attitudes. He might be spotted as an emperor, straddling his chair as if on horseback, defying the chastened horizon, conquered and annexed in advance. Next he would drape himself in a toga (of any stripe), gird his brow with foliage, and adopt a pensive air. Then, plucking a fig leaf from his laurel wreath (bindweed, actually), unclad, muscles bulging, he would painfully erect himself as a discobolus (but feverish the next day, and too sore to defend his honor in the Olympic stadium). Often, too, Crab would plant himself beside a road, arms outstretched, giving a slight tilt to his thorny head (for the bindweed prospered in his father's ill-kept garden), an expression of infinite mercy on his face.

11

Later, while remaining in the sculptural idiom, Crab thought of simplifying the task of historians and other pilgrims to come by leaving a trace of his passage everywhere he went. His first step was to adorn the garden gate of his boyhood home with a commemorative plaque; he went on to grace similarly the façades of hotels in which he had spent the night, so as to immortalize the event—and the innkeeper would have a second surprise soon after Crab's departure when, climbing the stairs to clean the room, he discovered a red velvet rope henceforth blocking all access to it, with a peremptory placard requesting visitors to touch nothing. Schools and hospitals frequented by Crab received his bust, with instructions to display it prominently in the lobby.

This, then, is the origin of those innumerable statues still standing at the corner of every street and alley, in open country, even in remote villages that no one has ever left: so many statues, and all of them depicting Crab in person, though no one would ever have thought it, for he died in abject anonymity many long years ago. This, then, is the identity of that absolute unknown whose name is indelibly etched on the façades of old apartment buildings—whom passersby suppose to have been a king, and privately mourn the passing of the golden age that was his history-free reign—or a musician—and music, they say, meant something in those days—or a poet—and where would literature be today without the inspiration of his glorious words?—or a painter—the last of the greats—or a scholar—and what scholarship!—or a revolutionary—if only they had listened!—or a prefect—concerned less with his career than with the daily life of the little people—or a national hero—and we could surely use a few more men of that caliber today.

Crab's name has gone down in history, that is a fact. But exactly when, impossible to say.

12 The task that Crab's biographer had set for himself was to be a long and arduous one. He knew it, too; he knew full well what he was letting himself in for. This book would keep him busy for at least five years, maybe more. But no biography of Crab had ever been undertaken—not one profile, not one study, not even the slightest fascicule—and this oversight desperately required correction. This would, therefore, be a complete and exhaustive biography, leaving nothing in the dark and nothing to chance; total objectivity would be its watchword.

He would begin by assembling the requisite documents, personal reminiscences, all the scattered pieces of the puzzle. There would be many places to visit: Crab's boyhood home—the very theater of his childhood (a theater peopled by marionettes manipulated by great heavy hands)—as well as the surrounding countryside. Then a nurse might possibly be unearthed, or, more likely, a putative foster brother, maybe a few surviving schoolteachers, former classmates and fellow soldiers, the far-flung family, the family friends, the neighbors, the first woman in his life—an octogenarian lass—then the next, and so on, right up to the most recent. The biographer further hoped somehow to reconstitute the paternal library, or at least its forbidden shelves. He would write to each of the relevant administrative offices—hospital, school, army, prison, among others—demanding any files relating to Crab. Next he would collect the sparse correspondence. Then he would set out on Crab's trail, following his path all across the globe in order to soak in every landscape, every milieu; in his wake he would negotiate deserts, oceans, distant cities, alpine footpaths, he would wear Crab's footprints on his feet, he would tread the selfsame trail. This preliminary inquiry would last, yes, five years at least, but only thus could his biography of Crab, solidly grounded, faithful to the smallest nocturnal detail, unassailable, become the definitive reference work that we so urgently need today.

He was forced to abandon the project, however, at the end of the first day, having discovered that Crab had been born dead.

13 Crab's godmother placed in his crib an almanac containing one page for each day of Crab's life. In the beginning, Crab ended each day by conscientiously tearing out and tossing aside one page, but then he began to tear out two or three pages at a time for the fun of it; furthermore, he sometimes went weeks without touching the book, out of laziness, or spite, or playfulness, or simple negligence. As a result, he no longer has the faintest idea how far along he really is. He might have died yesterday or the day before.

Not having heard the weatherman's report of the intense cold wave and incessant rain sweeping the country, Crab goes out in short sleeves and enjoys a long afternoon of balmy sunshine, out of ignorance, precisely. He might at least make some minimal sort of effort to stay informed about what's going on.

The same darkness once again answers the day's unchanging question. Crab feels his way to his bed. Stretched out on his back, he contemplates the moon outside (for what he sees is surely not the bull's-eye window in his bedroom rolling its lynxlike pupil). He fixes his gaze on it, obstinately, unblinking; with all his strength he concentrates upon it—his guiding light, his last patch of solid ground—in hopes of defending his thoughts against that old inward attraction, but once again it's no use.

Every night the same old chore: Crab horizontally re-lives the events of the day gone by. If he can see in their succession an indisputable logic, with everything—from the first morning light to this precise moment of recollec-tion—linking up perfectly in his mind, then at the end of the reel he will fall asleep. But if at any given point something sticks, if some troubling detail resurfaces and tangles the straight line, then Crab has a very hard night ahead of him. On the assumption that every effect has a cause, he works to discover the origin of the incident in question, which forces him to reexamine the preceding events, which in turn begin to seem in themselves quite mysterious, then completely incomprehensible, as were, come to think of it, those of the day before as well—and Crab, abandoning all hope of elucidating anything at all, moves further and further back: his own past be-gins to look extremely unlikely, more improbable than the future, the few memories he is able to recall and to classify are probably no less illusory than the supposed re-mains from which paleontologists reconstruct the world (how admirable their manly self-assurance!) but which have in fact always existed underground just as they are now, like any other mineral, marble, say, or porphyry, which no serious archaeologist would dare catalog as ves-tiges of some castle or antediluvian temple.

In the end, Crab begins to wonder if he has ever lived. His scars evoke no past experiences. Nor does his navel. He refutes his memories one by one, showing them not to be his, proving their fraudulence with all the surli-ness of those experts who challenge the authenticity of Leonardo's paintings—every year they bring to light a few more erroneous attributions (the pride of the impostor); one by one they rip the pages from the catalog of his works; if this continues, they will soon be forced to declare that Leonardo da Vinci never painted a picture in his life, and even, pushing ever onward in their courageous enterprise of demystification, that he never existed, that his father and grandfather are fictional characters, as are all his ancestors, that Vinci is an imaginary town, Italy a land found only in legends, the Earth an unlikely planet, and only then, in the limbo of a nullified universe, does Crab manage to get to sleep.

And, for instance, Crab has absolutely no memory of his own birth. It is only on the strength of his mother's reminiscence that he can claim with certainty to have been born, that he is indeed of this world, and very much alive. But can he trust her story? His mother has deceived him so often. This wouldn't be the first time she's stretched the truth. Crab wants to believe her, but he wouldn't say no to some more tangible kind of evidence.

Since this morning, Crab has forced himself to observe the following regimen: he bites the nails of his left hand when he is apprehensive, and the nails of his right hand when he is burning with impatience. In this way, he will learn his true nature. Gloomy or enthusiastic, worried or fervid, anxious or optimistic: by this evening, the condition of his two hands will tell him who he really is; he will finally cease to be an enigma to himself.

14

Accordingly, he will forge a definitive mask, either beatific or wretched, but unshakable, shielded from passing moods, no longer dumbfounded by pleasant or unpleasant developments, by surprise or terror, a mask of boiled leather that will project the truest possible image of him beyond any possibility of dissimulation, precluding both forced smiles and crocodile tears; all will be able to judge him by his appearance.

But it is not yet noon, and all ten fingers are bleeding.

Crab cannot understand it, he has just counted the hairs on his head three times and come up with three different numbers. It's no easy task, knowing oneself intimately. Bald people have a tremendous advantage there. Of course, if you know one bald person you know them all. Crab, on the other hand, is a very mysterious person, very hirsute. Nevertheless, he persists, he wants the truth, he starts again—one, two, three . . .

15 This ridiculous misunderstanding arose, stupidly, from a moment of inattention as the announcements were being written up. Thus the small circle of close friends invited to Crab's christening found themselves in the church where his memorial services were being held; meanwhile, the funeral procession was entering another church with quiet dignity just as the priest was blessing the union of Crab and his young bride, and just as another group, gathered in a third church to welcome the wedding party, gazed with astonishment at little Crab wrapped in a blanket and suspended over the baptismal font, clearly in no hurry to put an end to his bachelorhood, squirming and squalling like a condemned soul.

They can laugh about it today—but at the time grief tugged at every heart.

The Pyramids will outlive Crab, but will they bear witness to his passage on this Earth? How to be sure?

You wouldn't think it to look at him, but Crab is doing his best to become a man, a real one. A man in every sense of the word. A complete man.

Alas, he has only a vague and fragmentary conception of the nature of this important personage; his half-amused, half-appalled contemplation of his own body—by turns burning with desire, racked by hunger, blue with cold—tells him precious little in the end; each of those states is only one discrete aspect of a single subject as observed from a given point of view. What he wants is to grasp the full complexity of man with just one look. But man is never fully himself, not even when desire, cold, and hunger lay claim to him all at once. Crab intends, therefore, to study him in each of his states, every face, every timid but potentially limitless variation determined by age, sex, race, and other fashions, by the changing seasons, by deterioration, by surgery.

Conscientious in the extreme—you know him—Crab personally enters into each of these countless avatars, he incarnates them indiscriminately, all of them simultaneously, an inconceivable man and yet the only true one, whole, entire of himself, representing all humanity, at once old man and expectant mother, pretty little big bald redheaded skinny seven-year-old, with jet-black hair and the graying beard of an athletic, hairless, and quite obese patriarch, wearing thick glasses, with a baritone voice, a perfectly aquiline snub nose, a Greek profile and a penetrating gaze, naked but for a feather loincloth, bundled up against the cold. . . . Gritting his teeth, Crab assumes the body of this martyr.

No sooner has he set foot in the street than he finds

that he has gone too far, beyond all hope of solidarity with his fellows; he is as alone as ever, surrounded by men who are not men, who are scarcely men, flimsy approximations of men, unfinished, half beast, childishly stubborn little minds, affected apes, dubious characters, clumsy customers, dabblers, stiff-jointed amateurs, all neophytes compared to him — him so naturally mechanical, so masterly, exemplary in every way, from every angle: a figurehead, a model to be distributed throughout the schools and the stars, along with a frog, a plane-tree leaf, and a quartz crystal.

Crab watches his figure. Neither smokes nor drinks. He is maintaining himself for the long run. He would never admit it, but his secret hope is to hold on until the end of the world.

But some time later, one morning, leaping out of bed, Crab had an unpleasant surprise: his legs were missing, vanished, from thigh to foot. He was shaken, dimly sensing that this was going to complicate his life in one way or another.

17

His left hand had also been amputated during the night, unbeknownst to him, but Crab did not notice it at first. In fact, he remains unaware of it even today, three weeks after the operation. Let us not forget for a moment that Crab, in the strictest possible sense, does not work. His right hand is quite sufficient for day-to-day operations. He will, of course, eventually discover that he no longer has a left hand, but only by chance. One day or another, offhandedly, he will find out. Come to think of it, given his lack of unambiguous memories of that hand working or grasping, he might even doubt that he had ever had a left hand, and then he will have no difficulty convincing himself that one hand is far better than two for a man such as he (after all, he gets along well enough and badly enough with just one head)—and so he will cut off an ear, poke out an eye, thus enabling himself to direct all his attention toward one precise point with greater ease and efficiency, and all thanks to his newly streamlined equipment, simple to operate, compact, and thus permitting immediate on-the-spot intervention without the dangers of distraction, confusion, or loss of focus that plague the more elaborate instrumentation available to a healthy body—an instrumentation which so often proves unnecessarily complex given the tiny events it is called upon to deal with.

That said, the surgeons might at least have left Crab

one of his legs, the left or the right, whichever would have suited them.

In this condition, crippled, half bedridden, how can you begrudge Crab his subtlety? It is his wind-borne kite. He continually unwinds the string, yes, but he holds the spool tight. Will not let go.

Crab was born in a prison, a sordid dungeon in fact. His mother was incarcerated there for reasons that still elude him.

18

Several years went by, for his mother had been given a stiff sentence. Finally, one morning, the guard opened the door of the dungeon and announced that the prisoner was free to go.

"Not you, you stay," he added, shoving Crab back inside. His mother shrugged limply to signify powerlessness and gave him a sad little smile as she closed the door behind her.

Crab bristled; for what reason and by what right had they kept him locked away here since his birth? But the warden answered that there had been a considerable decline in the number of misdeeds and murders in the area since Crab's birth and throughout the whole of his vile existence behind those walls, a drop so precipitous it could not be put down to mere coincidence. In vain Crab reminded him that he had not yet been born when those crimes were committed—it's no easy thing to provide proof of or eyewitnesses to your non-existence. He was advised to reconsider his defense strategy. He pleaded guilty and justice was done; he was sentenced to life imprisonment amid heartfelt applause. The crowd left the courtroom wearing smiles of satisfaction. There was a palpable sense of relief in the air. People like that Crab fellow were made for a life behind bars.

It's not painful in itself—to tell the truth you don't feel anything at all—but it grips you, it constrains you, it robs you of a multitude of pleasures, there's no way to move when, like Crab, your foot is stuck between land and sky because you were unlucky enough to be there at the precise moment they came together, their edges snugly joining to form that one perfect circle; you will spend the rest of your life at the horizon. After a few failed attempts— laughable or pathetic, it's never easy to say—Crab has given up trying to free himself. He will grow old there.

Crab had a stomachache all day yesterday, abdominal cramps. It had been quite some time since he'd last had a stomachache, abdominal cramps. So obviously, one day or another, he would once again have a stomachache, once again suffer those abdominal cramps that tormented him yesterday, all day.

19

Crab is feeling better this morning, but his alarm clock is broken and didn't go off. It had been quite some time since Crab's alarm clock had last been broken. So obviously, one day or another, it would once again break.

Crab is running very late. He puts a pan of milk on the stove and attends to his ablutive splashings, forgetting to keep an eye on the milk, which boils over; this had not happened to Crab for quite some time, so obviously, one day or another, his milk would once again boil over.

Now Crab is running down the street; he trips on his untied shoelace and sprawls headlong into the plates and cups displayed along the sidewalk in front of a china shop; his nose is bleeding, the sleeve of his coat is torn, a thug makes off with his wallet, he can't find his glasses, the shopkeeper demands that he pay for the damage, the policeman who has been called to the scene asks to see his papers, and Crab, unable to produce them, is hauled off to the station for further questioning, then locked away in a cell from which, as night falls, his lawyer finally has him freed; but after all it had been a long time since Crab had last stepped on his shoelace, had a nosebleed, torn his clothes, lost his glasses, broken dishes; nothing had been stolen from him lately and he had not had to deal with the police for quite some time, so obviously, one day or another, he would once again step on his shoelace, have a nosebleed, tear his clothes, lose his glasses, break dishes, have his wallet stolen, and be dragged off unceremoniously to the police station.

But in accordance with this principle, which governs his entire existence, and given the fact that up to now he has never enjoyed one single moment's peace, Crab believes that he deserves a full day of rest tomorrow. A reasonable request. It will have to wait. It's simply been too long since Crab was last tormented by his rheumatism. And there are other experiences he has yet to go through, experiences that count for something in the destiny of a man, and of which he has so far inexplicably been deprived. There are plans for a house fire. An unhappy passion is set to gnaw at his heart. He will step on the tail of a snake (a more elaborate variation on the shoelace theme). He will soon be hearing from a mysterious blackmailer. He will lose a son. His car will roll over three times. And after all that, if Crab were once again to be racked with his abdominal cramps, it would not be at all surprising after such a long respite.

Crab was supposed to die of cancer. The doctors gave him two months. Then he was run over by a bus. The best laid plans . . .

And it seems that Crab is not the most wretched of men.

Do not be surprised if one day you see Crab walking toward you with a resolute gait, not running or digging in his heels, but rather slowly, even cautiously, as if he were crossing a frozen pond, not looking at his feet, though, nor feeling his way along the landscape with the toe of his shoe, but on the contrary with a firm, even step, as if he were walking on grass or a plush carpet, not sinking in, though, on the contrary, with a certain haste, a perceptible haste restrained with some difficulty by sheer force of will—itself perceptible—like a fakir who takes his time crossing the hot coals, hearing clinking noises all around him and imagining that he is walking on a gold mine—do not be surprised if Crab, having finally come face to face with you, gazes at you with a pensive air, neither insistently nor insolently, though, on the contrary, rather discreetly, covertly, as if he were waiting for you to give him some kind of sign, some reaction, so that he might know exactly how he was supposed to deal with you, neither questioning you nor trying to capture your attention, though, on the contrary, fleeing if by chance you should happen to speak or make eye contact, but remaining as long as you say nothing, as long as you keep still, making no sudden movements that might frighten him off, as long as you appear indifferent, distracted, distant, even disdainful, as long as you seem not even to notice his presence, or not to care about it—do not be surprised if Crab then gently closes your eyes, for he has every reason to believe that you are dead.

20

At first glance, Crab does not look the part of an assassin; rather, this lithe young artist seems more the compassionate and forgiving type. But to make such an assumption would be to misunderstand certain of his qualities. The ten fingers of a pianist make up the two hands of a strangler. Crab will not go on allowing himself to be humiliated forever without reacting.

Crab would like to lash out as well—to give a few saber blows of his own—but he is not at liberty to do so; his most urgent task is always to fend off the attacks aimed at him.

In fact, the most common criticism leveled at Crab is that he spent too much time in the company of his mother—that awful woman—during his childhood.

Crab spent most of his schooldays walking down hallways, following the traffic flow, as it is mistakenly called, as if it flowed sinuously to the sea, lined by willows, poplars, aspens, when in fact it only leads straight ahead until it reaches other equally obstructed hallways, for all the hallways in the world run together, forming a tightly interlaced grid, a network paved with tile or linoleum, with no exit, broken only by the occasional classroom, dormitory, refectory, and—all too rarely—the calm, clean infirmary where it is so nice to suffer a while.

Strangely, whenever he tries to think back on that period of his life, a period full of little boys running after each other, among whom he tries to identify his, the one he was—his only lead being a bad photograph, blurry, shaky, as if produced by an unwieldy paintbrush (his only lead, because he has no memory of the face he bore at that age, when mirrors were for fogging up or passing through)—each time he fixes his studious gaze on those children, scrutinizing them one by one (his photo in one hand, and in the other a pointed chin that never turns out to be his own), Crab hastily concludes that he has chosen the wrong school and turns away in disappointment, concerned for the child's welfare, so preoccupied that he blindly passes by the establishment's only exit, thus entering and finding himself trapped in its inextricable labyrinth (to use an adjective that is itself irremediably caught in the trap).

He is well and truly lost by the time he notices his oversight. How to leave this place? He tries to retrace his steps but succeeds only in losing his own trail. Nothing looks familiar. His terror alone sticks close by him, a little too close. A long and loving embrace. He searches through his pockets and extracts an unfiltered cigarette—impeccably rolled, soft, smooth, compact—which he brings mechanically to his lips but does not light.

Now a child appears in the distance, eyes lowered, running in his direction, tearing down the hall (but dreaming of the magical sense imparted to that phrase by the mind of Baron Haussmann), yet with an increasingly halting gait—and that man keeps staring at him, sucking on a stick of chalk, then finally stops him and asks huskily how to get to the exit.

"Don't ask me," answers Crab. "I'm looking for it myself. Will you let go of me? You're twisting my chin. You people make me sick with your filthy fixations. Filthy pederastic nostalgia. I must run into creeps like you two or three times every day. When I grow up I'm going to grow a greasy beard and never set foot in here again. You wouldn't by any chance happen to have a real cigarette for me, would you?"

Nipped in the bud, Crab will die on the vine.

Other people's grandmothers are a horrible sight, Crab realizes once again as he passes through the long, overcrowded wards of the rest home, a bouquet in his hand; thus he walks quickly, trying to avoid looking too much from side to side, straight to the armchair where he

48

knows he will find her, and then swoops down, lifts up, squeezes mightily, and covers with kisses the figure of a mummified witch who stinks and prickles and squints and drools, that strangely beautiful old siren, losing her hair by the handful, her yellow hair, his good old grandmother, sprightly as ever.

22 Crab was dying of boredom. Travel, the theater, nothing could entertain him. The stimulants his doctors prescribed had no effect. He stopped eating. Chewing is not so bad at first, but it soon becomes tiresome. His strength ebbed.

If a swimmer who ceases his agitations immediately sinks like a stone, thought Crab, then the earth should open up beneath my feet, for I hereby give up. An ideal death: the ground gives way, and the body, too tired to continue, is buried erect, planted deep, without ceremony, whereupon calm returns to the surface and every trace of this lightning-fast interment disappears under the grass.

But even death could not arouse Crab's curiosity. The prospect of eternal life is of little comfort to someone who finds every moment unbearable. And the great void that others promised him was scarcely more enticing— what less has it to offer than mere emptiness? Crab had emptiness coming out his ears; he had a shrunken bellyful of it.

He was forced to take to his bed. Summoned once again, the doctors could only confirm their futile diagnosis. Crab was dying of boredom. All their learning was in vain.

Then someone had the idea of calling to his bedside a master clockmaker, who saved him.

But Crab will never be completely cured. While they are never quite as serious as his first attack, there are frequent relapses. Boredom still wakes him up in the middle of the night from time to time.

Crab does what he can. He gets out of bed, puts on

some music, pours himself a drink, picks up a book, lights his pipe—and boredom offers him a comfortable chair. Crab struggles to hoist himself out of it.

He climbs the stairs to his studio. Boredom is a solid thing, three dimensions, pure matter, an ideal medium for a sculptor—but what's the use? sighs Crab, and he drops his hammer and chisel.

Bonbons, says Crab—*cui bono? cui bono?*

23 Crab paged through his appointment book and replied that no, alas, to his deep regret, he could not make it to the party; he had made other plans for that night: to stay home all alone and have a really shitty time.

Despite everything written about him—his wildness, his escapades, his sudden mood swings, his flashes-in-the-pan, his about-faces, retractions, rapid-fire conversions, on-the-spot transformations, his volatile nature, Crab is a creature of habit. You will never find him straying from his habits, no more than a statue straying from its pose. He sticks close to them from morning to night. Crab kills time slowly, over a low flame, as if he were flaking off each second with tooth and nail; not a single one escapes him. He goes through a watch a day.

To be sure, it was not ever thus. For many long years, Crab held the conviction that time was not to be used. Look but don't touch. He stepped aside when it passed by. How to climb aboard that moving train, coming from who knows where, bound for an equally uncertain terminus? Crab would not make the trip. Some of his days stretched out to great lengths, sometimes even overflowing into the next by dint of insomnia—at such times the clocks have nothing left to grind, their hands spin fruitlessly until a real night of deep, dark sleep reestablishes the rhythm of time's passage. Then the rhythm would go off track again, and this time the days flashed by like lightning bolts in a night with no way out.

Sometimes Crab aged ten years in a few hours, and

then he would stay stuck for centuries: time passed beside him, over his head or between his legs, it carried off his friends and left him standing, burdened with all the world's boredom. Crab did not have a single contemporary; he was always either their ancestor or their last-born child. Each time he made admirable efforts to adapt. He adopted the customs of the moment, he bowed down, fit in, slipped into place (for the only appropriate way to speak of man in society is with the language of stockboys), he accepted the mockery of Crusaders on horseback, made merry by his tunic and buskins. All for nothing. Just as an undercurrent sometimes randomly hoists up a swimmer and casts him onto the reefs while all those around him continue to splash about in a glassy sea, an acceleration of time suddenly propelled him, and him alone, into the middle of a gathering of powdered folk, all fans and lace, while he was dressed in filthy overalls, a monkey-wrench in his hands, and once again there was laughter and derision. Always behind the times, Crab is, or too advanced, never up-to-date, a laughingstock passed down from father to son, from generation to generation.

Finally, he managed to master time by creating habits for himself, one for each second of the day, from sunrise to nightfall.

Now he repeats himself tirelessly, he replicates. He walks in his own footprints, same shoe size, same speed, same path, he moves in a series of painstakingly precise gestures, like those of an artisan at his task, no matter what he is doing, as mechanical as the sun in China, exactitude incarnate, his feet on the tracks and his head in orbit, and the heavens bear the shining trace of his hair.

It's nothing special, but this watch fills Crab with pride. Crab claims to be nothing more or less than time's accomplice, ensuring that it passes unhindered, and thus equally accountable for its crimes, like the driver of the getaway car who leaves his motor running while the others pillage and murder in utter tranquillity.

But Crab is once again overstating his importance, as is proven by that selfsame watch, whose underside is his own terrified pulse.

There was a time, between his fifteenth and twentieth years, when Crab would scrawl out a brief letter every night, explaining his decision to get it over with and obliterate himself in sleep. He would place it prominently on the bedside table before turning out the lights and tear it up when he awoke. There was no lack of good reasons, the day gone by always provided him with a wealth of motives, never quite the same as those the day before, and no justification for clinging to life.

Crab would feel a strange and rather agreeable sensation as he drafted those melancholy notes, and little by little, almost unawares, he began to concentrate on their form and their style. And then things changed; it became impossible to get any sleep, he was forever turning the lamp back on so he could emend or delete an awkward turn of phrase, he would stay up all night long, writing with increasing fervor, and what had been a little note became a long and eloquent letter of farewell, more closely and more convincingly argued, but in the end invalidated by the intoxication it betrayed, the brio of the text giving the lie to its content (just as a violinist's only reason for moaning and wailing seems to be that his brightly-polished shoes are too tight).

From then on, Crab gave up trying to find oblivion in sleep. At night, he wrote. Drunk on caffeine, his exhaustion did not trouble him for long. He would join it in bed at dawn, just for a few hours. Then he would get up, go out, and walk with a resolute step, hoping to face his problems. It never took long. Winter, malaise, cruel blows to the jaw, the undisguised amusement of women he encountered—and when it wasn't the rain, it was the

24

wind that came snarling after him. At dusk, when he decided to go home, humiliated, beaten, shivering, Crab had enough material to write all night.

Crab swallows a cherry whole, with the pit. It was a suicide attempt, but no one will believe it.

Crab is hoping to hire a poet for his small-to-middling business. Two applicants show up. The first enters, his open hand outstretched, his forearm firm, his smile wide, his eye sharp, his stride ample; he plants himself solidly in the armchair Crab offers him. After him, the second enters, his feet impede his slow progress, he offers Crab a hand (but only on the understanding that he will return it), hesitates to sit, finally alights formlessly on the edge of the armchair, and his gaze fills with eyelashes.

Crab deduces

—that the first is a straightforward lout, devoid of subtlety, mystery, finesse, an opaque and irksome dullard, a foamhead, a self-important ape, a complete athlete, a power tool, a brute who mistakes his bull neck for an unexpressed idea and his pointed shirt collar for the wings of progress, just another self-confidence man, incapable of producing anything but oil. Oafish characters! Polluters!

—that the second is a delicate soul who fits the bill.

Crab leaves sentences behind him, a frail wake testifying to his recent passage, but he is no longer there, he is long gone, and their curious meanders, their multiple detours are simply the path of his zigzag flight, revealing his effort—thus far unrewarded—to break the thread that he unwinds behind him as he advances, no matter what he does, no matter where he goes, his struggle to finally break free of that trail of ink, thanks to which he would be pursued and apprehended were he not fortunately much quicker than his reader; but fatigue will rear its head one day, he will slow down, his reader will fall upon him. He is advised to stop writing and lay low for a while; the trail will soon fade. Of course. Crab would only have to give up moving. But since writing is his only means of motion, the slightest shadow of a gesture would set the bloodthirsty pack on his tail again.

His tongue encountered something hard. "I've found the ring in the Candlemas cake," he cried naively—but no, it was the baited hook.

With no assistance from anyone, Crab drew up the plans for his house. He picked out the stones at the quarry and shaped them. He cut down trees in the forest for the frame. He gathered together all the necessary materials. He dug the foundations. He mixed the cement. He raised the walls. He put up a three-story staircase. He covered the whole thing with a roof. He did the plaster, the woodwork. He installed the plumbing, the electricity. He hung the wallpaper, laid the carpet. He furnished each room according to his taste. He climbed the stairs. He entered his bedroom. He threw himself out the window.

Crab is writing the following little text in the public library, with no other intention than to offer his lovely table mate the spectacle of a poet in action—thus from time to time he sits with his pencil suspended between heaven and earth, between the eternal and the abyss, and allows himself a long moment of idle meditation, but then suddenly, as if inspired, obeying some incontrovertible order from on high, he bends over his notebook and writes out this very sentence, feverishly, with the slightest of smiles on his lips, a smile of quiet satisfaction, which soon becomes a skeptical pout, and then an ugly grimace of disgust, and Crab fiercely scratches out the last few words and recopies them verbatim, feverishly, with the slightest of smiles on his lips, a smile of quiet satisfaction, all the while miming the ardor of a fresh, brow-furrowing inspiration, and then he lifts his pencil again, he runs an agitated hand through his hair, he favors the world around him with a vague glance, noticing as he does so that his spectacular act has indeed impressed his table mate, since she has her nose buried in a thick book on Italian Renaissance painting, trying to make an impression herself, obviously, you can see it in the way she turns the pages, the way she lingers over every reproduction with feigned emotion, takes hurried notes, quickly checks her watch, thrusts her pen and her notebook into her bag, puts on her coat, leaves the book lying open on the table, and runs toward the exit. But Crab doesn't care, he has effortlessly filled up his page thanks to her, his workday is done.

Crab screws an awning to his umbrella and goes out.

26

If everyone was like Crab, no more blows, no more caresses, but bodies avoiding each other, shadows ringed
with iron. Many balances and scales take no notice of his
existence, even the most excitable ones, those that twitch
nervously at the merest glimpse of the hirsute, red-eyed
prospector, gray with grime, clutching three grams of
gold dust in his fist.

Nevertheless, Crab is there, on the lookout, ready to
intervene; he wants nothing so much as the chance to
enter the service of a passion, an idea, as a simple valet,
handyman, charwoman, beast of burden, whatever; to
which he would be entirely devoted, giving of his blood,
his kidneys, his lungs, and his time; for which he would
bend over backward and keep going; which he would
rather be cut into pieces than betray, into tiny pieces,
whittled into shavings; for the defense of which he would
make of his body a rampart, spewing molten lead from
every orifice.

But Crab never quite manages to make himself useful.
Every time, he is passed over in favor of another, more
motivated candidate. And Crab returns to his comrades,
for he is not the only volunteer to be snubbed; he
has gradually grown close to this perpetually sidelined
crowd—quivering in a petrified infinitive—who might
be called upon one day, but who have nothing to read in
the meantime.

How to occupy this pointless, idling body, what to do

with this head running on empty? Work must be found for the former, distractions for the latter. Thus Crab spends the majority of his time boxing his own ears.

On the other hand—and this is not meant as a reproach, but facts are facts—we must recognize that Crab irreparably ruins everything he touches. Except plaster, however, which runs through his fingers.

If only he knew how to talk to plants: a cactus is an orange tree to which he has sung a lullaby.

Crab flees in every direction. He slips away in front, he vanishes behind. He takes himself off. He declines the offer. He avoids the subject. He plays possum. He skips a turn. He steps out for a moment. He takes his leave. He crosses over. He runs for cover. He saws at the branch on which he sits, hoping to make himself a beautiful wooden coffin.

27 Crab did his best to blend into the crowd like everyone else. It was not as easy as he had imagined. To his way of thinking, the crowd was by definition open to all; make your way to any spot where others swarm and you become ipso facto—as they used to say in the Forum—an adherent, an active participant, a member in good standing, a fixture.

So he dipped one foot, then two feet into the moving crowd, churning with countercurrents—a Mediterranean sea setting out despite itself to cross the Atlantic—but whose fluctuations seemed to obey a rigorous system of rules that Crab was upsetting, despite or because of his average size: sometimes he towered head and shoulders over an assembly of dwarves; sometimes, on the contrary, his chin was pummelled by the oncomers' knees; thus he shrank abruptly, then rose to the surface again, then shrank once again without missing a beat, never on the same level, always comically out of step, as if chance had nothing to do with the comings and goings of the crowd, as if they were governed by traffic rules of which he, Crab, was unaware; finally he managed to extract himself from the mob—after a long walk through a forest of legs, under a sky heavy with sad fractured moons—thanks to yet another sudden collapse of the giants surrounding him.

Ever since that day, Crab sticks to the walls. His pet lizard follows or precedes him, tugging at its leash. They cross vast fields of ivy and wisteria, billboard landscapes yellowed by the sun or grayed by the slow sinuous rain rolling drop by drop from the rooftops; they slog through that pink mud toward the bare wooden palisade, where other dangers await them—splinters bury themselves in Crab's hand or cheek, or in the delicate, palpitating belly of the lizard—until finally they reach the sheer, high walls that constitute their surface of choice: it is true that brick tends to be grimy (the whitewash will take care of that), and that some run-down façades either crumble beneath them or (if they have just been painted) are marred by the trace of their passage—either way, it is hard on Crab's already threadbare jacket and the more precious but also more resilient jerkin of the lizard—but at least they are keeping their distance from the crowd.

The only real danger stems from those encounters that Crab and his lizard cannot avoid: when other pedestrians of their ilk, skimming the walls in the opposite direction, suddenly pull out in front of them. No one wants to yield the right-of-way, and for good reason: the slightest side step onto the pavement would thrust the heedless walker into the path of the oncoming crowd, plunging him back into that eddy of perpetual panic where no two feet are ever headed in the same direction, to be tossed about and jerked around as if he were standing upright on the surface of the ocean, to be reminded once again that there will never be a place nor a path for him in this swarming throng where onrushes, exoduses, sallies, and retreats compete for space and cancel each other out. Confrontation between Crab and the oncomer is inevitable. Each jockeys to hug the wall more closely and struggles to push the other aside. They fight with one arm and one leg; the other two limbs remain glued to the wall so as not to open a space into which the adversary might swiftly slip his foot and thereby gain a decisive advantage.

So far, Crab and his lizard have always emerged victorious from these encounters (painful rituals, all the same); their reputation is such that many wall skimmers choose to avoid confrontation by veering off or suddenly shifting into reverse. They are quite right to do so.

It turns out that Crab's lizard is nothing less than a crocodile. Crab was carelessly holding his opera glasses the wrong way around.

Far from upsetting or alarming him, this discovery fills him with delight; far from screaming or struggling as the crocodile opens its mouth to swallow him, he slides in with enthusiasm and even a sort of sensuality — as if he were squirming feet first into a warm bed — and luxuriates within the animal's entrails. He will be quite comfortable there. A safe haven at last. How could anyone not feel protected in this capsule, clearly designed to hold a man, custom tailored — the length is right, and the width too — and endowed with mobility to boot? It is a sheath of Damascened scales, open to all, lined with pink swan-skin to soften the blows, resistant to water among other things and impossible to break into without quite a struggle. Anyone who tries to make off with it has an unpleasant surprise in store. Its occupant, lying prone, will have no difficulty drifting off to sleep. Mosquitoes pose no threat. Oxygen is regularly recirculated, nourishment punctually provided at mealtimes: meat and fish.

This is now Crab's chosen mode of travel, without cost, without danger, without fatigue; he follows the Ganges, the Mekong, the Nile, the Limpopo. But he is irritated to find that the secret of reptilian locomotion—which he had hoped to keep entirely to himself—is already out, and that numerous tourists in gavials or alligators have already preceded him along the banks of those great rivers.

28 Crab latches his suitcases. Off to America, immense America, it is time for Crab to visit America. He has been told that no one can turn their back on America anymore. And Crab has never set foot in America. None of his many voyages throughout the world has yet led him to America. He is seriously lacking in knowledge of America. This earns him the jeers of his contemporaries, and sometimes even insults and blows. Until now, a vague uneasiness held him back whenever he considered undertaking this expedition, a doubt, a suspicion, perhaps a premonition that America was not a place for him. He always backed off.

This time, his mind is made up. He's going. He has latched his suitcases. He is leaving for America. The trip only takes a few hours nowadays, thanks to the development of air travel. An aerial bridge, as permanent and solid as a Roman viaduct, links the old continent with America. The craft takes off gently. Now Crab is floating above the clouds. The age-old comparison with sheep still holds and is in fact more apropos than ever, since, from this bird's-eye view, as seems logical, one does not see their legs, whereas a ground-based observation forces the poet into bad faith if he wishes to maintain his simile, unless he imagines the entire flock of sheep flipped over on their backs, a wholly unnatural position that itself must somehow be explained, probably by the irruption of a wolf into this bucolic scene. Below them, the ocean scintillates, a lovely spectacle, it scintillates, it glistens, absolutely splendid, yes, it scintillates, a bit monotonously perhaps, it scintillates as far as the eye can see and the hours go by and still there is no land in sight;

Crab senses the mounting apprehension of the steward-esses, and then of the passengers, which soon becomes a real panic, and finally the first officer announces that they have just enough fuel to turn around and go home; that the plane has drifted off course, the navigational instruments must have malfunctioned, the airline will find another plane for you right away.

Meanwhile, an atmosphere of extreme perplexity hangs over the nation's airports. Twelve airplanes had set off for America that day, and all have met with the same fate, while no anomalies were reported on the other routes. Tests confirmed that the onboard instruments were in perfect working order, thus ruling out the possibility of sabotage; and since it is difficult to believe that twelve senior pilots and their twelve copilots could all have drifted off course through incompetence or inattention, all flights to America will be suspended until the mystery is resolved.

But Crab has always dreamt of taking a sea cruise. The ship he eventually boards is, in fact, an extremely luxurious steamship. The dolphins build arches as high and as regular as those of a Roman aqueduct between the old continent and America. The crossing comes off without incident. All the same, the American seacoast should have emerged from the mist long ago, and when the passengers, troubled by the immensity of the Atlantic, begin to openly express their dismay to the captain, he is forced to admit that this is a mystery to him as well, for the ship is currently in the middle of the Pacific and Siberia will soon be in sight.

Back on the old continent again, Crab learns that

a series of expeditions are being planned, all aiming to discover the route to America—lost, forgotten—and thereby to reestablish the relationship and the mutual exchange that have greatly enriched our lives for the past five centuries.

Crab is no dupe. He has never seriously believed in the existence of America, that legendary land invented by tellers of tales in a last-ditch attempt to make themselves interesting to others, a land given credence by the recognition of sovereigns aiming to distract their subjects from misery and boredom—the twin fomenters of revolution—and to boast of supposed diplomatic successes, thus justifying their position of power at no cost to themselves. Similarly, any indecisions or missteps apparent in their policies could be explained away by the heedlessness, the instability, or the omnipotence of the powers that be in that faraway land.

America!

There is no doubt that Crab's name will be forever linked to the discovery of this astounding hoax.

It dawns on Crab that the great war being fought over there on the other side of the world, devastating landscapes and decimating populations, concerns none other than himself, Crab; that he is the center of the conflict and even its sole cause. And he is sincerely, profoundly sorry. He never wanted it to come to this.

Through an inheritance, Crab became the owner of an immense desert, but only on the condition that he swear never to sell it, never to alter it, never to set foot in it. None of which prevents him from feeling quite at home there.

"This is my future home. It's still under construction, but I moved in yesterday. It's already inhabitable, so there was no point in waiting. As you see, most of the work is already done," adds Crab, nonetheless gesturing toward a vast empty lot bearing not the slightest trace of habitation. But to those who express their misgivings and try to convince him that construction has not yet begun, he replies, "The entry and exit are there, all the windows too, wide open; the rest is a luxury that I can very well do without. The Philosopher carries his roof in his head," he adds. Then he stretches out flat on the ground, flat under the sky, and goes to sleep.

Crab is the last of the sages; his body, unfettered by desire, has no object other than to age, to age without a break, straight to the end.

But night is blind and careless with time. To put it more precisely, night simply does not participate in the world's orderly advancement and progress. The ingenuity of men does nothing for her, or against her, not the untouchable night. Only day is moved by their decisions. For night takes no notice; she ignores any change that has occurred since the beginning, notably Crab's intellectual evolution. To her, things remain as they have always been. Crab discovers this upon awakening. Rosy-fingered dawn rises between his thighs. He is hungry. Not easy to be young, never a moment's peace.

Earth turns to dust, or mud; water either freezes or evaporates; air burns the lungs and causes colds; the wind that musses your hair is nonetheless as filthy as an old comb —but, unless Crab is mistaken, fire is always itself, identical to itself, faithful to itself, intransigent, incorruptible, inalienable, unwaveringly hostile to compromise. Only fire can be trusted. Fire alone. So Crab will go and live in fire. He will be quite comfortable there.

Thus Crab moves out for good without having to leave his house—an unsound hovel, uninhabitable, like some derelict windmill left to grind the chaff of abandonment and oblivion. It only takes one match, with its simple little flame like the single candle on an infant's birthday cake, to give the place a flamboyant new decor. It is as if fire had been lurking in a corner, hoping for a chance to climb the curtains. But do not call fire a wallflower, for that would offend this gregarious soul; rather, it was biding its time, as latent as a wildcat. It was waiting for its moment. Fire likes to appear at windows, would have no difficulty upstaging a pope in the middle of an address to the gathered masses, even one who goes up in flames himself and becomes a human torch in an attempt to steal fire's thunder.

The windowpanes shatter. Fire stretches out its long limbs, immediately makes its presence felt, takes up all available space, acts as if it owned the place—quite at home, already cramped for space—it clears out the cumbersome furniture, undertakes a ruinous renovation, takes out walls, ingeniously brings the three floors together in one; the fireplace smokes naively, the weathervane spins around like a chicken with its head cut off, the flames bedeck the dormer windows, red, orange, or yellow, each one in turn is hunted down by the others and led to the stake, where they stand up straight and tall, like a condemned witch who curses you all, ignoble judges, flaccid priests, stiffnecked priests, fat faces of the gathered gawkers, ludicrous asses, and proudly offers to Merciful Satan not only her asbestos soul but also the dead wood of her long thin limbs, the sulfurous locks of her crackling hair, and the ten blue sparks flying off her nails.

This is precisely the decor Crab had dreamt of. He runs joyously from one room to the next. How lovely. Surely the most beautiful fire he has ever visited. He retraces his steps, he discovers new features every time, wonderful transformations unsullied by tasteless extravagance or ostentation. And so convenient. Never again the insistent foot in the door. Just you try and sell him a Bible now. Nor will boredom find a home here—his tiniest knickknacks dance merrily in the flames. It is probably not as comfortable as it could be, but Crab cares little for comfort; so many benefits, so much grandeur are surely worth the trouble of the occasional burn.

30 Crab will never understand why, even though their legs are two or three times longer, their waist more willowy—and then there's that neck that just won't quit—women are generally smaller than men. And that is only one example. In fact, Crab understands absolutely nothing about women. To begin with, he doesn't understand a damn word they say. He speaks several languages with ease, but his fluency in Chinese is no help to him when faced with a Chinese woman. Nor do their gestures help him to grasp the sense of their words. When a woman motions toward a chair, he raises his eyebrows in surprise, thanks her just in case, and leaves the room carrying this odd and cumbersome gift. When she motions toward her bed, he calls in the movers.

It should be clear that Crab's relationships with women suffer as a result of this ongoing misunderstanding. So he thought it might be a good idea to hire a translator, who follows him everywhere and repeats to him—in exactly the same words—their every utterance, after which he turns back toward them to pass on Crab's response (for it must be pointed out that women are equally deaf to his words). But in no way could this be called a mutual incomprehension, since mutuality implies an intimate relationship and, more than that, the existence of a genuine connection, an exchange of amorous correspondence, an erotic complicity, in short, a shared tumultuous past, of which Crab, for one, has no memory.

Should we pity him? Certain strange phenomena, observed many times, lead us to believe that Crab's painful situation would only grow more complicated—would in fact become utterly intolerable—if he somehow succeeded in overcoming this linguistic handicap. For instance: when he is caught up in a fast-moving crowd and happens to touch a woman, however fleetingly, there results a small explosion accompanied by acrid smoke, startling both of them (although Crab is used to it by now). Equally disconcerting—and no less inevitable—is the short circuit provoked by this brief contact, which affects all the surrounding electrical fittings, plunging the entire city into darkness.

How would Crab dare approach a woman in these circumstances, knowing that his saliva, when mixed with that of another, immediately produces coal; that his fingers, when interlaced with those of another, can never be unknotted, that his breath bleaches hair, that his caresses give frostbite to elephants, that his lips suck out every last drop of marrow?

Be that as it may, Crab—patient, attentive, a shrewd teacher, always ready to play and to tell stories—would make an excellent father.

That absent-minded man picking wildflowers in a field is in fact pulling off the heads of young girls in a schoolyard. You recognize him, of course, it's him, it's Crab; he is going to be beside himself with embarrassment when he realizes the enormity of his mistake—what will people think of him, with that huge bouquet under his arm and no vase large enough to hold it?

31

Accustomed—through natural inclination or otherwise —to slip his gaze under skirts, Crab discovers, to his great discomfiture, that the people who sell leopard-jaw panties are making a killing.

🦀

At first, Crab believes he sees a cloud of butterflies fluttering around her, blue, gray, some of them black; but they are eyes popped out of their sockets, in thrall to the irresistible attraction of her haunches—blinking satellites, some colliding with others, some, having grown too bold, snuffed out between her thumb and index finger, only to be immediately replaced by others, traveling through space, skirting intervening bodies and obstacles, piercing the muslin curtains, falling like hail from upper-story windows or spit out from air ducts like bullets from a rifle, springing two by two out of passersby, blue, green, and black eyes—each with its gleam—and Crab has to lower his lids to prevent his own eyes from striking out on their own for a closer look, for the girl is now passing directly in front of him on two legs whose rivalry is as intense as that of Miss Norway and Miss Finland: too close to call. A soft leather leash is wrapped three times around her wrist, as if to bind together a little more securely that delicate bundle of green veins; at the other end of the leash wobbles an unhealthily fat and eczematous little dog, legs twisted, pinkish belly bristling with teats (valves, perhaps, through which one might reinflate the wretched animal should the need arise), snorting or sniffing with a sound of rustling leaves, its black, slapping snout slathered with snot and saliva, and then suddenly, in a yawn gaping like an ugly wound, revealing rotting gums sparsely sown with teeth less rich in ivory than in ebony (to continue the African metaphor), as well as a mauve tongue so thoroughly chewed that it must have completely lost its flavor, then finally closing its mouth, more or less, and relieving itself without lifting a leg— in its pants, so to speak—thereby forcing the attendant nymph to come to a standstill. The opportunity is not to be missed. If he doesn't try his luck, Crab will regret it for as long as he lives. All right, here goes. He draws near. Brazenly, he comes straight to the point, "I have a male—could we make little ones?"

Every beautiful woman Crab meets has on her head one hair of the woman he secretly yearns for.

32

This, in the end, is the question. Where is Crab more likely to run into the woman he so longs to see again: in the crowds strolling the boulevards, or on some deserted square, some vast unfrequented esplanade? After all, it takes many people to constitute a crowd—so many that she might well be one of them—so, in any case, she is surely more likely to be there, among those thousands of people, than in a place where almost no one ever goes, yes of course, but how to spot her among those thousands of people, it would be nothing short of a miracle if he found her, if he stumbled onto her, her specifically, among those thousands of people, whereas in a place where almost no one ever goes, if by chance she did happen to come along, Crab could not miss her, he would certainly see her, yes of course, but it would be nothing short of a miracle if she happened to be there, her, why her, her specifically, in this place where almost no one ever goes?

Crab wavers between these two strategies, opts for one, abandons it immediately, overcome by doubt; opts for the other, but, overcome by doubt, abandons it immediately; once again examines their respective strengths and weaknesses but reaches no decision; desperate to find the best possible solution, he paces back and forth in his room, vowing not to leave until he is certain that the plan he finally settles upon is indisputably the right one.

Having accepted the fact that the female sexual organ is in fact what has always been misnamed the right ear (and vice versa), having accepted and recognized this fact,

Crab gets an eyeful as he walks down the street. He doesn't miss a second of the show.

33 Crab had, after all, told him so. Crab had warned him that it would be a headache. Crab did not hesitate to express puzzlement — "Why don't you get a dog or a goldfish instead?" The other guy would have none of it. And now that his hippopotamus has locked itself in the bathroom, the other guy asks him to help break down the door! He even tries to tell him that's what friends are for! Crab finds it a bit much.

Come to mention it, he has never found friendship to be anything but a source of sorrow and disappointment.

By chance, Crab runs into an old friend, unchanged by the passing years.

"Still the same, it would appear?"

"As you see. You, on the other hand . . . wait, don't tell me . . . have you had your arms cut off?"

"That's right, but are you sure we haven't seen each other since then?"

"I don't think so. Oh well, maybe so."

Crab bitterly regrets having introduced his friend Onan to his friend Narcissus. What an awful idea. Those two are birds of a feather, he thought. How wrong he was. Those two have absolutely nothing to say to one another. A painful evening. They completely ignored each other. You can imagine what it was like. Each in his corner. And Crab having to keep the conversation alive all by himself.

78

Crab lives with an absent wife. And she is the sweetest and kindest of absent wives, and the most charming by far. In all honesty, of all the women he has never seen, she is the one whose absence torments him the most cruelly. Crab wouldn't change places with anyone. This love casts a radiant glow over his life. He is the happiest man on earth.

34

Crab and his absent wife make a remarkably harmonious and well-matched pair—which is not to say that they are one of those couples who complement each other only insofar as she has leprosy and he the plague. Their passion retains all the vitality of their very first days together. Never one word louder than another, never a quarrel—and yet they have lost none of their autonomy and do not hesitate to show it now and then. But not for them the wretched business of adultery and the torments of jealousy. They trust each other implicitly. Why should they seek elsewhere what they can find in their own home? Crab even rejects out of hand the possibility of an extramarital life after death. How utterly idiotic all that is—pap from priests. They will be buried together, the same day, in the same hole, and they would never dream of leaving it.

Crab and his absent wife have started a family. Crab has a real weakness for his absent children. You won't catch him wielding the rod or the flail nor raising his voice. Besides, Crab's absent children are absolutely adorable, easy-going, obedient, good as gold, little angels forever hiding behind their mother's skirts.

Crab is a happy man.

They brought him the head of his wife, which they had found under a bush; but until the legs are found Crab will not give up hope: "Maybe she just needed to get away for a while."

Make no mistake about Crab's erections. His desire for justice far outweighs any others he might feel. But, having at his disposal no other erectile organ than the one standing between his legs, Crab has learned to make do, to make the best of it. This penis, carefully graduated in accordance with the metric system currently in effect, has offered him a more complete knowledge of the nature of his desires and the opportunity to classify them in order of priority.

35

In this way, Crab discovered the marked preeminence of his desire for justice, since in that context his penis reached a height of 8,848 meters, which incidentally is precisely the altitude of Mount Everest, the topmost point on the globe.

But in fact, Crab has twice surpassed this record. The first time, in the course of one of those episodes of public merrymaking dictated by the calendar, he saw his desire for solitude suddenly climb to 9,000 meters. On another occasion, his desire to leave his mark upon the moon proved even more insistent, since he did indeed leave his mark, and the altitude of 384,400 kilometers measured that night no doubt constitutes the upper limit of Crab's elasticity.

But we must discount these two exceptions. Under normal conditions, his desire for solitude rarely surpasses 7,000 meters. As for his desire to leave his mark upon the moon, it faded as soon as it had been satisfied and disappointed. Not a day goes by, on the other hand, that Crab's deep-rooted desire for justice does not make itself felt in the most urgent manner.

As a conclusion to this scabrous chapter, there follows a list (derived from measurements daily taken by Crab himself over the course of a year) of the average dimensions attained by some of his most pressing desires: desire for silence, 6,708 meters. For music, 6,707 meters. For happiness, 474 meters. For a good bed, 85 meters (with a spike at 2,000 meters). For a good fire, 39 meters. For a good book, 6 meters. For a good bath, ditto. For death, 2 meters (the chart shows a sawtooth form). For love, finally, 17 centimeters (neither more nor less, never. The only constant observed. Should be considered a standard). The latter is to our knowledge the lowest level attained. Lesser desires no doubt exist within Crab, but they remain vague, secret, latent, unspoken, or submerged, and therefore undetectable to the rudimentary instrument by which he measures them.

A local movie theater was to screen his life. This was something Crab just couldn't miss. His life in its entirety, absolutely uncut, without elliptical fades or dissolves — how such an uncompromising work could have made it past the censors and the ratings board, Crab did not know; he was really very surprised. For this film must surely consist of nothing but the most unbearably intense visuals, an unbroken series of blood-soaked, pornographic, sacrilegious scenes. A hell of a show, of course, but what rawness, what violence! And how could the censors have failed to grasp the subversive nature, the affront to the established order, to public morality, inherent in the hero's every word and underscored by his gestures? Those blistering rejoinders, those exhortations to upheaval — from Crab's earliest days onward. Such a film would horrify countless hearts, countless stomachs, countless souls. Every community organization in the country would demand that it be banned immediately. They would sooner poke their children's eyes out. But it will be too late: the winds of this radical dissent will carry the flame to the highest heavens. The Universe is ripe for expansion!

There was no line at the ticket booth. No one in the theater either. The lights went out; the show began. Crab fell asleep as soon as the first images began to appear. It was the usherette who woke him up. He asked if he could stay for the next showing. Since there were no other potential customers in sight, she let him stay. And the second showing began.

Crab rarely leaves before the end, but this time he fled the theater after only a few minutes, so dull, so insipid was the show, so talky and yet so inaudible, badly acted to boot, and numbingly slow. Low budget, and not a penny's worth of imagination. On his way out, he wasn't surprised to see that they were already removing the title from the marquee.

Crab was born with his brain where his heart should be, and vice versa; they expected great things of him, and at the same time they feared the worst; but it soon became clear that this reversal changed nothing, and when at twenty he expressed a desire to go into administration, many lost all interest in his case.

There's no point in keeping it a secret any longer: all his life, Crab was a wholly insignificant individual devoid of charm or personality, whose elementary vocabulary still included far too many words and expressions for his inane thoughts, so that he often spoke completely at cross-purposes and made himself ridiculous. Fortunately for him, no one paid the slightest attention to what he said. Crab passed unnoticed. He walked arm in arm with his shadow. He was one of those people who make up the masses. He resembled his neighbor like a brother; he even resembled his brother's neighbor. His doubles filled the streets; Crab couldn't help but smile every time he encountered one of them, so astonishing was the resemblance of this bystander to one or another of his friends. Crab was born to fill out crowds, to elongate waiting lines, to occupy functionaries—he was himself a functionary, and punctual, zealous as a spinning wheel, supervising the free circulation of illnesses, yawns, and proverbs. Neither good nor evil, but simply bound for purgatory, neither large nor small, ordinarily ordinary, eternally in between, graying body and soul, and at the mercy of the stroke of an eraser—indeed, that was the only conceivable end for Crab, death seemed far too spectacular and extreme a phenomenon for him, disproportionate to his existence (like launching an air assault against a fly, in the guise of an old slipper); the drab, plotless life he slowly unreeled was simply not worthy of such a sensational denouement.

Ah, but Crab had a gift.

Crab had an inestimable gift that lifted him out of mediocrity. Crab was a photographic genius, without a doubt the greatest the world has ever known. His eye, his instinctive sense of light, his intimate acquaintance with shadow, the infinite patience with which he observed his fellow men, his contemporaries, awaiting the moment when their nerves force their impenetrable faces into an ephemeral self-portrait (and what their faces refused to give away, their hands eagerly offered him), his lust for discovering in every clumsy, vulgar arrangement, every overfamiliar or inhospitable landscape, some hidden marvel, invisible to three eyes out of four, and deftly bringing it to light, so that it alone shone forth from the darkness that surrounded it—the concentration of these many talents made of Crab a photographer that no one, try as they might, will ever equal.

Death—which is not fooled by appearances and knew just what it was doing—carried him off one cold night in 1821.

(The following year, having smeared a copper plate with Judean pitch and exposed it in a dark room, Nicéphore Niepce invented photography.)

Confused, unsure where to put or what to do with his hands, Crab mechanically thrusts them into the pockets of his trousers, his jacket, or his overcoat. The result is that whenever he needs them for one purpose or another, he has to search through all his pockets at great length before he finds them. When he finds them. When he doesn't find his feet instead.

Sad but true: Crab has few answers at his disposal. Summoned to express his opinion on a given question, the only point he makes is blank; he fades away. No longer exists, died yesterday, is on a slow boat to China. People turn away from him with disdain.

Only then springs to his lips the cutting reply that would have muzzled all those cocksure blatherers. But it is too late, the hostess has shown her guests out; Crab stands alone on the staircase where his wit, grown limber, leaps like a musketeer. How many times, after a particularly pitiful showing at a dinner party, has he found himself caught between two floors with a melodious piano in his arms! How many times has he slyly and cleverly spit on the bannister! But without witnesses, without an audience: he alone was aware of this belated triumph, whereas his shame, known to all, spread inexorably through the night.

This cannot be allowed to continue. Crab knows what to do.

From now on, he will spend every night preparing the next day's retorts and repartee. He will write it all down. Thus he will put an end to the awkward silences, the stuttering, the banalities, the defensive pleasantries. And if Crab's rejoinders seem slightly incongruous, or off the subject, or even absolutely off the wall, he will nonetheless be admired for his original way of thinking and his constant drive to push back the limits of the conversation.

Tomorrow, for example and for starters, the first person who greets Crab in the café where he daily dips his croissant will hear the following reply, delivered tit for tat: "The cat is a vertebrate but doesn't know it . . . keep it under your hat. . . ."

Whereupon Crab will empty his cup with one gulp and be on his way.

All the same, Crab prefers not to get involved in conversations. He will merely furnish the reference to a relevant passage from among his endless writings, a passage dealing with the very subject under debate, thoroughly encompassing the question and settling it once and for all. You need only look it up. You will not get another word out of him.

Crab is not impressed by the vast ocean, with its sharks, its typhoons, its submerged islands, its waves higher than a house. The ocean cannot put anything over on him. He stares at it unblinking, hands on hips, in a defiant pose, and addresses it curtly: "Pass the salt, old Ocean."

The preliminary work was painful, Crab admits it; he really sweated over it. More than anything else, it was terribly time-consuming. Neither dangerous nor particularly difficult, mind you, more like child's play or homework; Crab never had to leave his table, his patience alone was tested. He worked quickly, following an infallible method, both simple and effective, nonetheless requiring close attention and great discipline. Crab kept up the pace, but it was an enormous task, involving, in this first stage, the combination of every word listed in the dictionary, in every possible permutation. He stolidly settled down to this thankless job. It will come as no surprise to learn that he devoted many years to this project, to the detriment of all others.

Crab took the words individually, as distributed by alphabetical order; each word was combined with the next, in every possible manner and in all possible declensions, then combined with the word after; next combined with the latter and the one before; combined with a third; with that one and the two preceding ones; with that one and the first alone; with that one and the second alone; with a fourth, and so on. Crab copied all this onto large sheets of paper, and each page, duly filled up and numbered, was added to the stack piled on the carpet. He was soon forced to take out the ceiling and then to make a sizable opening in the roof.

But one night it was all done. The manuscript was as tall as a mountain. Crab had to hoist himself up to the summit in order to finally begin the second stage of the project, a rather more delicate operation, not so much because of the danger of falling as because of the very

38

nature of the work to be created, a masterwork, the book to end all books, after which the world would enter upon an epoch of meditative silence—for what more is there to say? what is there to add?—and man would spend the rest of his days reading and rereading these pages, nodding his head.

Crab had a wealth of material at his disposal, containing every book that has ever been or ever will be, and not only every book but also every daily newspaper, letter, list, speech, conversation, owner's manual for machines yet to be invented, catalog, police report, administrative white paper, not to mention the myriad unpublished manuscripts that his method had spontaneously produced: an incalculable number of novels, epics, poems in free or rhymed verse, biographies authorized or otherwise, scandalous diaries, conflicting scriptures, encyclopedias, treatises as diverse as they are multiplicitous (economic, scientific, historical, political). . . . Crab had only to cull certain choice fragments from his mountain in order to give birth to an impressive personal *oeuvre*, whose paternity could indisputably be traced to him alone.

But no, his project was more ambitious still. He had something much bigger in mind. So Crab began to cross out sentences, whole passages that he found meaningless, or mediocre, or that he had already read elsewhere; he made massive cuts, burned stacks of pages that he deemed unworthy of him, sparing a word here and there, hacking away with a pair of scissors, ripping up ream after ream, and finally saving only the cream of the original manuscript, a hundred or so essential pages of aston-

ishing extracts from that dense, obscure summa, that un-
readable intermingling of banalities and incoherencies:
yes, that was how Crab wrote his book—and he doesn't
believe it would be possible to go about it any other way.

39

That day Crab was taken seriously for the first time. He usually had no difficulty getting past security. His moronic air worked in his favor, and the guards' suspicion was always directed elsewhere. He would leave the premises unhindered, with a leisurely gait—too much haste would attract attention, as would too much offhandedness, but he took care not to whistle—and walked right past the guards—nothing to see here—and on through a series of wary patrol squads searching everyone but him. No one ever gave him a second glance at roadblocks; they waved him on, move along, on your way. He obeyed, secretly delighted, passing by a long line of parked cars whose occupants were undergoing endless interrogations. Crab could have crossed a border with every step and never run into difficulties. But he had no desire to flee, no one suspected him, he could come and go as he pleased, he was in no danger.

But that day they got him. He was walking in the street, wearing his long overcoat, his face a picture of innocence and his arms swinging free, as usual, when suddenly he was taken seriously, immediately surrounded, and quickly subdued. He made no resistance and later, in court, denied nothing.

Now Crab would like to know, just to set his mind at rest, precisely what it was that caused his downfall. Something got past him, but what: a word, a gesture? He gave himself away, but when, how? For pity's sake, someone tell him where he went wrong.

Even today, Crab cannot speak of his incarceration without a shiver. Sometimes this memory even wakes him up
at night. He has to go out for a breath of air to regain his
composure.

His space was severely restricted. There was a line he
could not cross upon pain of death, a horrible death, a
slow asphyxiation. It isn't easy to imagine such things
today. You have to have lived through them.

Locked in: an excruciating sensation, unbearable.
Crab crashed into the walls like an insect; he walked in
circles in search of some unlikely escape route, a tunnel,
a vertical chute, a ladder high enough to get him out of
there. He soon found himself back where he began. At
such times he lost all hope. He would lie motionless for
days at a time. Why bother to move? No matter what he
did, he was caught in the trap, dead in his tracks.

Then he would get up, suffocating, his chest tight. He
would tear open his collar. He would scream. He was
a fearsome sight. He would start flailing about again,
throwing himself against the walls. He would take other
trains, other airplanes, other boats, he would once again,
in vain, circle the closed space—510,101,000 square kilometers—that had been allotted him, a space surrounded
by pure emptiness, what an awful time that was.

Moonshot, marshot, venushot, jupitershot, mercury-
shot, saturnshot, uranushot, neptuneshot, plutoshot—
Crab constitutes the whole of the Department of Ter-
minology at the Center for Aeronautic and Aerospace

40

Studies, and quite a chore it is, too. He is forging the vocabulary of conquest.

No one would like to see a climate of competition take hold here—that would serve little purpose—and of course it would be a serious mistake to judge the merit of a given worker on the single, rather petty criterion of efficiency, and yet the figures speak for themselves: it is quite obvious that Crab's work is proceeding much more rapidly than that of his engineer and astronaut colleagues. In point of fact, Crab has already finished the job—entomb, enmoon, enmars, envenus, enjupiter, enmercury, ensaturn, enuranus, enneptune, empluto: this final list marks the end of his indispensable lexicon.

But alas, thanks to the continual missteps, the laziness, or the incompetence of Crab's technician colleagues, the beginning of this very promising expedition must be deferred time and time again.

The blade plunges down his throat, glides upward under his chin, carefully skims the rugged contours of his jaw, refuses a kiss from his hypocritical lips, slips under his nose, slides into his cheek as if it were soft butter, effortlessly, encounters his cheekbone and skirts it, swiftly, driving before it a foamy blue-gray wave, sprinkled with long and short whiskers, that, breaking, leaves behind it the violet conch of a malformed ear; the blade then plunges back down Crab's throat, and this time the blood slithers out of its hole; the wounded hero picks up his fallen weapon and resumes the painful advance; gripping his face in his left hand, he pulls and stretches his skin; despite the blood flowing down his neck, he somehow finds the strength to push across the temporary plains thus created—the fragile rope bridge holds up as he sprints over the gaping chasm, giving way the moment he sets foot on the opposite bank: he can't go back so he goes on, clutching his weapon in his fist, penetrating still deeper into the undergrowth of his beard, until he reaches the ear—yet another—from which he immediately turns away, diving into the brushy hair, then completely shaving the skull that houses it so imperfectly, and he follows through on his thrust, pursues his breakthrough, shaving the rug under his feet—why stop when everything is going so smoothly? Crab steps into the street, razor in hand. This morning is not like the rest (which never quite seem to recover from the dusk of the day before); this is a morning full of promise, a new day dawning.

Crab's eyes are the two thumbs of a sculptor, and everything is grist for their mill, everything is clay; the world changes wherever they fix their gaze—if they fix on you, you too will change. A flurry of sharp, forceful glances to begin with, in order to smooth out the material, whatever it may be. No material is too hard or too resistant; in the end each works out to be very much the same, just as easily kneaded, just as easily shaped. It all comes down to imposing a new way of seeing. Crab's eyes make the necessary modifications, his gaze grows more penetrating or more enveloping according to the material at hand: it sculpts the rhinoceros, remodels the hippopotamus. It digs, it delves into the arid immensity of the sea—those horses you see among the waves are his doing. The cutout silhouettes in the clouds are his; they change expression according to his whim and disintegrate the moment he turns his back. The city undergoes the same transformations: angles are undone, made round, surfaces are polished, vistas overturned, masses crushed, lines softened, a return to horizontality; and then Crab's gaze comes to rest on the passersby, and, retouching their faces with great care—an overly insistent gaze might break the bridge of a nose, tear off an ear, or poke out an eye, and indeed, alas, this has occurred on more than one occasion—he strengthens features, ovalizes heads (simultaneously freeing them from their drab shroud of hair and reestablishing them against a glowing backdrop), slims and elongates bodies, melting the excess fat that had them all joined at the hips, restoring to each silhouette its own discrete errancy, as empty spaces hurry to fill in the cold air thus emptied (cold being the only form of emptiness our senses can perceive)—Crab himself trembles from head to toe, the whole thing threatens to fall apart: he closes his eyes just in time to prevent it.

How many times will he have to fold the sky to make it fit into his pocket? Crab is ready to go. He fills trunks, boxes, crates. He is getting ready to move, and it's quite a job. This is his chance to rid himself of useless things, dusty mementos that have ceased to commemorate whatever they once did, having reverted to the hideous, vulgar trinkets they were before a sorceress, passing through the souvenir shop, transformed them into nostalgic pelts and herself inexplicably disappeared. Crab will not take it all with him—out of the question. A major sorting through is in order. But the sky, for instance, he can't leave the sky behind.

And once he has managed to fold it, what pocket is he to put it in? That's another problem. In his trouser pocket, like a handkerchief? Then what would he do with his handkerchief? The other pocket is already full of sand: Crab couldn't leave the desert behind either. His inside jacket pocket, which has a hole in it, contains the precipices and ravines that make up the mountains, which he will certainly need some day; he knows himself well. Finally he slips the sky into his breast pocket, over his heart, like a gaily patterned but unobtrusive foulard —but the azure clashes with his charcoal-gray jacket, just as Mary's one blue dress clashed with the carpenter's overalls in the laundry hamper.

Next Crab rolls up the yards, the lawns, he makes a great pile of the land and loads it onto a wheelbarrow, he collects the sea in a barrel, he assembles his flock, the most ferocious ones in front—one last look to make sure he hasn't forgotten anything—and off he goes.

Firmly resolved once and for all to make a radical change in his life, Crab set off toward the church whose steeple soars above the roofs. He walked quickly despite violent gusts of wind; he struggled forward like a man swimming against a torrent, like a man digging a tunnel with his hands, like a man scaling a precipitous peak, like a man breaking down walls with his head, so firmly did the wind resist his progress. But this very struggle strengthened his resolve, inspiring Crab to new heights of fervor. There was still time to change his life. A gust carried off his hat, and Crab did nothing to catch it—what a symbol!—for a new man was being born, one who had little use for such futile protections. He shed his coat of his own accord, without missing a step, his eyes glued to that unshakable steeple, still fighting the furious wind, which seemed to want to thrust him back to square one, to force him back into the petty, gray life he led before the revelation. But no, those days were gone forever, Crab had opened his eyes. Finally he reached the parvis, and at that very moment the bells began to ring, as if for a baptism—what a symbol! Crab quickened his step, removing his gaze from the steeple, high and pointed as if designed to impale God Himself; he walked past the church, crossed the street, entered the travel agency whose sun-drenched posters he had spotted the day before, and without a second thought bought himself an airplane ticket for the islands.

For how can we believe even for a moment in the conversion of one such as Crab? Closing the door behind him, he raised his eyes to the weathervane placed atop the steeple. "Am I dreaming," he said, "or has that rooster laid a church?"

Let's get this straight. It is not so much our taste for red meat and green salads that distinguishes us from the animals (you will have recognized our friends the tiger and the snail), nor our careless rutting, nor our allegiance to those in power, nor our untapped reserves of courage that allow us to engage in battle—and then devour—an ailing dwarf; rather, it is the Gothic cathedral, for instance, that clearly expresses the nature of our originality: a tendency to complicate everything, to fiddle even in stone. That single inclination is the source of our peerless prestige among all the terrestrial masses.

Crab begs to differ. As always, he has good reasons.

By the greatest of chances, Crab has gained possession of ancient documents of unquestionable authenticity, according to which the centipede was once, at the dawn of time, a shrewd and subtle thinker, and the goose a great luminary; the buffalo's lectures attracted large crowds of bees and wrens; the flea had not yet taken to drink; the bear was a theologian by vocation, the cat a cosmographer, the orangutan played chess, the turtle dabbled in philosophy, the lobster toyed with politics. . . . But evolution continued, natural selection; in a world where life is experienced by the senses and maintained by force, each of these animals saw its intelligence shrink little by little, saw its mind grow dim, its memory and reason decline even as its agility improved, along with its particular

100

beauty, its natural grace, its instincts, its bounteous good health. Harmony was established at last, and only one straggler continues to disrupt it with his anxieties, his shames, his endlessly reiterated adolescences. Only man was unable to do away with his consciousness. Rather than providing for his defense and paralyzing his prey, his venom turns against him. Oh, it's a long, long road that separates this meticulous little wretch from the superior wisdom of the carp and the polyp. Crab himself remains far from his goal, and he knows it full well, but at least he is moving in the right direction. And the movement is irreversible. Crab grows more obtuse with each passing day—too slowly for his liking, of course, but nevertheless he is making progress. No sooner has he caught up with the monkey than he aims at becoming the equal of the ass. And the ass is only a stop along the way. Crab has already drawn alongside the seal. He has the ostrich in his sights.

Crab was born with webbed feet. His mother kept it a secret. His father beat him. His two brothers and two sisters mocked him cruelly. A sad childhood. But time passes. His parents died. The oldest brother made his career in the army, the other perished in an accident. The first sister married a former varsity shotputter, and the second opened a little shop selling regional specialties, now fallen on hard times. As for Crab, he became the majestic swan we all know and love.

43 In the old days, Crab used to see many potato bugs. He had only to bend down to see a potato bug. The potato bugs have abruptly disappeared from his life. Crab isn't asking for much; he only wants to know why. Granted, he had left his country house and moved to the city, but that could not possibly be the only explanation. There are surely other reasons, deeper, more secret, having to do with the shady machinations of some well-known figure: Crab loses his way in a maze of conjectures. In all honesty, he cannot accept the hypothesis that potato bugs have developed a personal grudge against him. He has always sided with them against the potato, finding it inconceivable that such a vegetable — pale under its crust of filth and constantly thirsty for hot water — should be held in more esteem than the precious, hand-painted coleopter. So why this disappearance? Crab is resolved to lead the investigation. He is somewhat apprehensive of what he might find, what awful truth. He must be ready for anything. But he will see it through to the bitter end; this mystery must be solved. The worst torture of all is not knowing.

It has also been a long time since Crab has seen a giraffe, or even the tiniest giraffelet. But that is not the same thing. It is a completely different matter. Crab knows where to find them. He is deliberately doing without. He willingly forgoes that pleasure; it is always a good idea to keep on hand a reason to live. And this long privation only feeds his desire. More than once, Crab has found himself drawn toward the zoo. Halfway there, he managed to get hold of himself, he had the strength to turn around. But his resistance is weakening, he knows that one day he will no longer be able to maintain control of his legs. Unless he resorts to breaking or binding them, he will have to give in. This is it. Crab is off. He jostles the passersby. Burns his bridges behind him. Scales the fences around the zoo. Immediately spots the towering heads. And then what joy! What larks!

Abandoned at birth, Crab was taken in by a she-wolf; he ran naked through the woods with his wolf-cub brothers; no less than cold and silence, his footprints were one with the snow, black flakes less numerous than the white ones, no doubt, but essential. His eyes pierced the darkness, were essential to the darkness. The moon gave him a halo of which he never boasted, but to which he was attached all the same. He would never have thought of going out without it. The she-wolf still nursed him, more of a docile ewe than one would think, a good mother. Then he developed a taste for blood, which he would have happily drunk at the teat, changing none of his habits, and everyone would have been the better for it. But it's no use: rabbits always try to keep the secret of that bubbling spring to themselves, tucked away in the lining of their would-be mink coats; they run away with it, they hide under the bushes, one has no choice but to go after them. Thus his carnivorous instincts took root, and when the proper social service authorities, alerted at last, took the decision to remove him from that pernicious environment and to place him in the care of a hen, it was too late: Crab's adoptive mother made no more than a mouthful.

He was placed elsewhere. Then still elsewhere, for Crab devoured one mother after another. He devoured the otter, he devoured the sow and the doe.

Next Crab was placed into the care of a shrimp: kindness itself but as slippery and limpid as water. He thought he saw her everywhere, and his nascent filial affection was diluted throughout the vast ocean. A bee taught him table manners. A mare showed him the rudiments of the obstacle course. One after another, a garter snake, a magpie, a whale, a lioness, a cat, and an ant taught him all they knew. Others followed. Finally a bear took his education in hand with such firmness that Crab, still under her influence, continues to hibernate to this day, no matter how giddy he makes himself with coffee.

But these substitute mothers, however benevolent, devoted, and life-fostering, were unable to eliminate from his mind the idealized image of his natural mother. Worse, their teachings were sometimes contradictory, and that disturbed him: whom to believe? whom to trust?

Then his vague longing was finally realized: his repentant mother claimed him. She had readied an adorable little bedroom for him, with blue curtains. A tutor would help him catch up on the years of education he had missed. After a careful psychological evaluation, the proper social service authorities agreed to allow the young woman to take back her son on a trial basis. Thus Crab was returned to her, and his human education began.

Even today a gesture or a posture sometimes gives away his past: when he bucks, when he slithers. He has been known to spend two or three days as a parasite in the intestine of a cow now and then. These are not so much irrepressible resurgences of old habits as manifestations of his very natural desire to hold on to abilities and practices that he might need again someday in order to survive. You never know. We must not make too much of them.

44

And what's more, Crab always carries a heavy armchair on his back, for there is nothing so tiring as always carrying a heavy armchair on one's back, and he needs to sit down from time to time and take a break.

There is always more of Crab to discover.

Crab is as nearsighted as a squirrel — or was that little animal a mole?

His chin is firm, his gaze uncertain. It's up to his ears to decide.

Crab lets himself be led, he wanders, he flat-out refuses to climb either peaks or steps; he prefers to follow the curve. It is a fact: he has never climbed a single staircase. And yet every day he finds at least one descending staircase in his path. So Crab flows downhill, unhurriedly, without forcing himself in any way but rather out of a natural fluency — his particular knack for making like a ball and rolling ever onward. Passersby often pass him by, carried along by their momentum, but Crab's indifference shelters him from all phenomena resembling enthusiasm; he descends at his own speed, his hands in his pockets, along almost vertical inclines. Cyclists sweep past, crouched over their handlebars, hair and face set aflutter by the speed, but Crab remains above it all, an unchanging expression of indecision on his face. With measured gait, without precise destination (for where is there to go?), he moves forward by inclination alone.

There was the one controversial event, his birth. Since then, nothing. To be sure, there are others in this situation, but they are driven by hope, they are looking to the future, their time will come. The waiting room is packed. Finally you are shown into the study of a sinister magus who knows exactly how many days you have left to live, very few, but you will feel them as they pass—he removes a lung, a kidney, a heart, then shows you out—next! Crab is not there, he awaits nothing, no one; he does not wait, but spins out the hours.

Furthermore, the doctors already believe that he is dead—that he is already dead. He enters the conversation too rarely to shake their conviction; his pulse is too erratic. This man is dead, they repeat, his death occurred three or four years ago at least. Come, come. Crab is not living, undeniably, but does that really mean that he is dead? Crab himself is not sure. Maybe they're right after all. He palpates himself, then pinches himself. Hard to say. It would help if he had a scalpel. He drops his arms. He declines to offer an opinion. Neither for nor against the body lying there, heavy and diffuse at the same time. A sensitive nothingness. Nebulous. One hundred kilos of cramp.

Already half eaten by cats, or is that only an unpleasant impression?

Crab bursts into a department store.

"Four handkerchiefs, quickly, I'm bleeding, I'm sweating, I'm weeping, I'm coughing."

"Right this way, Sir. Are you sure I can't interest you in a shroud?"

It is a glue of the finest quality, really an excellent glue, no mistake, absolutely astonishing, glues any material with ease: cardboard and paper, of course, much as any glue glues, but it also glues leather, wood, stone, porcelain, cloth, plastic, metal, and it glues them instantly, definitively, and solidly, it glues what it touches once and for all, it glues and won't let go, glues and holds, glues water, fire, earth, glues the wind, glues the cold, glues the night, glues fear, a universal glue, tenacious, certainly the best of all possible glues, and it flows through Crab's veins— what has he got to complain about?

45

There is no way around it, Crab is ill; his head (which we have come to know so well) never used to look so much like a piano bench—but how can one be so careless, when one's name is Crab, as to stand in a draft while the woman next door is practicing her scales! He really should learn to look out for himself.

This is not the first time he has met with this kind of misadventure. Crab has grown used to such things. One spring, after an excessive inhalation of the odor of lilacs, he saw both his hands transformed into clusters of mauve flowers. And having lent an ear to a murmuring stream (would it not be just as accurate to call the clicking of a keychain in the pocket of a panting fat man a murmur?), he saw his two legs grow liquid and carve out two divergent streambeds in the prairie. Doubting Thomases will be allowed to inspect the stuffed head of a twelve-pound pike that Crab fished out of his left leg.

Crab is too sensitive. It will kill him one day.

Just last winter, unable to help overhearing the echoes of a domestic altercation in the apartment above (the wife wants a boy, but the husband is hot for a little girl), Crab found himself shivering uncontrollably, and his two knees knocked together with such force that they sank into each other, forming one enormous knee. The articulation continued to function normally and, apart from that great patellar knot, each leg retained its relative autonomy, its thigh and its calf. But as one might suppose, this sole exception to the rule of symmetry was enough to seriously affect Crab's ability to walk; he moved only by half-strides, tiny steps, and found it utterly impossible, among other things, to jump over puddles.

Such are Crab's headcolds—very annoying indeed.

Nonetheless, suicide is too radical a solution. All that Crab asks is to be rid of his head. He has no desire to give up long walks, for instance, or swimming or gardening. His greatest pleasure is to stretch out on the grass in the sun. The fleeting caress of a cat moves him as much as any love story (with its tender beginning and the small sorrow of parting that marks its conclusion), he asks for nothing more. And the head is quite useless in such matters, truly superfluous. It only gets in the way. No less intrusive than the head of a third party. Crab will have no difficulty doing without it. The head houses all manner of torments. It devises sad thoughts, fevers, lice, and more alkaline bitterness than the liver. It dwells on darkness. It always bites the hand that feeds it.

But as for doing away with himself, no. Crab hopes to have the courage to brandish his head on the end of a pike and to parade it through the streets, filthy old thing, among the spitting, cursing multitudes.

Take this hypothesis for what it's worth — coming from Crab, it should inspire prudence — but, true or false, we must agree with him that it has at least some basis in truth: Given the fact that it is possible to juxtapose anything with its opposite and thus to arrive at a definition by antithesis — good as opposed to evil, death as opposed to birth — should there not exist, in opposition to suicide, something like a deliberate and spontaneous self-generation? A diffuse, floating consciousness, a vague little soul, furtive as a cold draft, which might suddenly decide to incarnate itself, to take shape, to come into the world? This would finally explain why certain men seem so happy to be alive, so thoroughly at ease: they came into existence by choice. They chose the time and place. They gave themselves every advantage.

Crab, on the other hand, did not foresee the blessed event; even one day before it, he had no clue to the fatal outcome that was approaching. Crab was no more existent than all those others who will never exist, an innumerable legion in which he had his place, all bound for eternity—but we know what happened next. You will bear this name and you will drag this shadow. Crab never fully recovered from the shock. He has never really accepted the situation. Such incredible liberties they took with him. Hard time on terra firma, which forms its clods with its dead. Far too much sand in the desert's salt for hungry Crab. Far too much salt in the ocean's water for thirsty Crab. And then the constant irritating presence of oneself, right down to the end of the fingernails, and bloody battles on all sides.

Crab won't be difficult about dying. Death puts the hours back into the clocks. To die is suddenly never to have been born. Crab will be the first to forget his name. But he will not stretch out beneath a train—where do trains stop? He prefers to follow his shadow, which will gladly point him back the way he came. His seat is waiting for him, already empty. Killing yourself is like beating down an unlocked door. So says Crab.

112

Each passing day brings Crab one step further from the terrible day of his birth.

47

So comfortable, so carefree, so voluptuously inactive seems the existence of the cephalo—sorry, gastropod—mollusk, so little burdened by duties and responsibilities, that Crab, when questioned on his plans, makes no attempt to hide his intention to adopt that existence in the very near future. This admission never fails to raise an outcry. It's beneath the dignity of a human being, he is constantly told. You'll leave slime everywhere. Surely they don't expect to discourage him with that sort of argument.

The slug spews not from jealousy, nor from rage, nor from epilepsy; its liquid speaks louder than words, it is a froth that blooms languidly along the slug's sinuous path. And Crab is tired of leaving footprints behind him. From morning to night, without a break—barring the occasional, all-too-brief standstill—he must leave behind him, no matter what the season, in snow or in mud, the trace of his shoe upon the ground; with each step he must pit his body against the loose earth, sowing a row of footprints as he goes, and for nothing—they will never sprout, they will never mature into so many little Crabs. The only bulb that will be productively planted, at the very end of the journey, is the corpse of the sower.

As a trace of his passage on this earth, Crab prefers to leave not the simian outline of a foot but a discreet filigree on a cabbage leaf.

Then a more serious objection will be voiced: that he will find it difficult to bring his body into conformity with the customs of the gastropod mollusk, to mollify it, to effect the necessary retraction of limbs and head and thus attain the limp shapelessness, the remarkable elas-

114

ticity characteristic of slugs. But Crab has already solved that problem. His skeleton will encumber him no longer. He's going to spit out that bone.

Coat and shirt come off first. Then Crab thrusts his hand deep into his throat, grasps his left collarbone, and firmly but gently extracts it through his mouth. It all holds together. The entire carcass follows, except the skull, now more heavy and cumbersome than ever—but Crab, having taken a deep breath and placed his complicated brain in the temporary care of his simplifying stomach, has only to pull back his lips in order to shoot the obsolete dead man's head across the room.

The effect is immediate. Crab feels quite transformed. Not as swift, of course, but so much more supple. Laziness requires a specialized form of gymnastic skill inaccessible to dry, stiff, angular bodies, prone as they are to cramps and rheumatism, but rather reserved to the flaccid, the flexible, the unarticulated, the consenting. In this respect at least, Crab can already make a legitimate claim to being a mollusk, even if he still has a long road ahead of him before he becomes a true gastropod.

It was by dint of indolence that Crab became that sunken pile of sand with which you hope to make cement. Poor wretches, your constructions will not stand. Or with which you hope to make glass—the morning light will not pass through.

48 Doctors Parkinson and Alzheimer, weary of their fruit-less disputes—contradictory theoretical stances, diver-gent aesthetic choices, scholarly quarrels of no concern to ordinary men—have decided to rise above it all, to pool their knowledge and come together in a common pursuit, with a view to deciding once and for all just what constitutes a broken-down old geezer. Here comes Crab, thrust center stage, under the spotlight, cheered by some, hissed by others, officially recognized, at any rate, as the model to which all those who pass seventy years of age will henceforth have to conform.

But Crab has always been an old man, nothing new about that; he takes after his great-grandfather. The laws of heredity often hold such moving surprises for grieving families, who discover in the newborn the expressions and mannerisms of the ancestor who has been plucked from their affections, his gestures, his tics, as if it were yesterday, as if it were him, him yesterday, here today; the dear old fellow hasn't changed a bit, the head of the clan, the soul of the home, the founder of the proud lineage whose latest scion has just been born and who resembles him feature for feature, no mistake, the spitting image.

At birth, a premature little old man, weak, powerless, Crab already weighed no more than two and a half kilos. The nurse made what we must see as a very understand-able mistake: she removed him from the incubator and, after a stern talking-to, wheeled him back to the geriatric ward from which she thought he had escaped—"try that again, and I'll have you put away for good." Crab stayed put. He grew older, which obviously did not help to clear up the misunderstanding, quite the contrary, and the only thing troubling his caretakers was his extraordinary longevity; for while the patients around him usually passed away just a few days after their arrival, Crab inexplicably held on; the doctors were speechless to find him still alive every morning; it was even suggested, in hushed tones, that he might be immortal.

To hear him speak, though, Crab's condition was as hopeless as that of all the other goners. Having learned the language of men from the delirious ramblings of his fellow patients, he recited their desperate monologues verbatim, making them his own without understanding their meaning; in a distraught voice, he defied God, renounced his sons, called for his mother, cursed the merest shadow of a boss, pardoned a certain Louise, or Suzanne, for everything, evoked the names of a hundred women, tremulously formulated maxims, aphorisms, or chemical formulas (some of them wryly poetic), demanded to see a priest, a lawyer, hurry, recounted glorious or bloody episodes from an age gone by—all quite unmistakably the words of a dying man. He wasn't long for this world.

But the years went by, the cadaver in the next bed was changed three times a week, and the doctors succeeded each other in much the same way, as each reached the upper age limit. Sometimes they ended up in this very ward; pulling together their last bit of strength, they would beg Crab for his secret, for pity's sake, and Crab was only too happy to make a full confession: he had murdered a certain Suzanne, or Louise, committed an act of treason, buried a treasure, fathered a multitude of bastard children, tampered with the brakes in his boss's car, stolen Mademoiselle Portal's ribbon, and even, yes, broken Mademoiselle Lambercier's comb . . . but no one was listening.

One day the mystery was finally resolved. Someone came across an old register confirming the nurse's mistake, and Crab, now aged ninety-seven, reentered the incubator, where he was given round-the-clock intensive care, for the poor child was causing them all a great deal of worry, so weak, so sickly; no one knows today whether he was saved in the end or not.

Crab never forgets a single cemetery he's been buried in.

Now that the springs in his legs have broken, Crab does not so much walk as drag himself along. Some of them have poked through the skin of his thighs and calves. The slightest movement is sheer torture. If only Crab could brace himself on his arms—but that's out of the question. When misfortune sets her eye upon a man, she wants him all to herself. Have you ever seen a paralytic frozen in a sensual pose? Illness waits until he is sitting in an uncomfortable position before striking. Crab cannot count on his arms. The straw is already coming out in several places—the left elbow, the right shoulder.

49

Crab empties his pipe, gently knocking the inverted bowl against the edge of the ashtray, and as the ashes slowly pile up Crab's left leg grows shorter, it's a fact, and the ashtray and the coffee table soon disappear under the ashes that Crab—already quite diminished, ever diminishing, diminishing visibly—nevertheless continues to extract from his pipe; they form a carpet all around him, growing thicker, or deeper, by the minute, from which still protrudes one wriggling arm, or rather a forearm, a hand, two fingers shaking the last ashes from a pipe, light, gray ashes, light gray, covering the floor of this room, where you will find no trace of Crab or his pipe.

50 The certificate passes from hand to hand, everyone is eager to sign, they'd be ripping it from each others' grasp if they weren't afraid of tearing or crumpling it, which would mean putting the whole thing off, since that would require drawing up a new certificate and starting the whole process over again in order to recover the lost signatures, many years' accumulation come to naught — a disagreeable idea — so each takes great pains to treat it gently, a quick glance to ensure that there is no misunderstanding about the person involved (which would have troublesome consequences), then, fully aware of the gravity of their actions, they sign and pass it on to the next one, who does the same, the paper moves along quickly, several million signatures already, perhaps as many as three or four billion scribbled at the bottom of the form, specially printed for the occasion on an enormous roll of parchment, bound for Asia as soon as it returns from Africa, so that everyone, absolutely everyone will have signed Crab's BURIAL PERMIT.

Crab is laid out on his back, four candles burning at the four corners of his bed — "I'll be four tomorrow, too," a little boy whispers to him; receiving no reply, he climbs up on a chair and blows out the candles, then leaves, puzzled by Crab's unnatural silence, his long face, his pallor, his stiffness. But suddenly he understands, he understands as he catches sight of his mother, through the half-open kitchen door, pouring rat poison into his birthday cake.

Nowhere do more errors of tense occur than in utterances spoken around a deathbed. We speak of Crab as if he were still of this world, but soon the sad truth brutally forces itself upon us and our language grows muddled, confused, tries to confine itself to past tenses with such insistence that it might be referring to some antediluvian ancestor, the father of the monkey, whereas this cadaver is still warm, moist, and dreamy. Or else it's the opposite, the eulogies are carefully formulated in the imperfect tense — Crab was the best of us all — but then the emotion of the moment overpowers us, this cannot be, he cannot be dead — he who so loves books and birds — besides, it's his fault we're all suffering, as surely as if he were giving us a full-scale beating, doubling us over, throwing us to the ground, twisting our arms, tearing out fistfuls of hair in some cases; a dead man would never display such aggression. Of course, our pain, all too present, all too active, has reversed our perspective yet again, with a shudder we come to our senses, we start again — he who so loved books and birds. For a few minutes, we speak of Crab in the past, we nobly celebrate his memory, but it doesn't last, again the present and the imperfect vie for space on our lips, hold fast, nor does the future hang back, since our poor friend will live on in our memory.

Crab died absolutely alone, down and out, in the bleakest poverty. Many years have passed; his name has become glorious, and his circumstances have improved considerably.

For fear of being buried alive and waking in the tomb — which happens sometimes after a pessimistic diagnosis — Crab had his carcass incinerated, so that when he finally awoke from the comatose torpor that had mistakenly been deemed definitive, he was only a pile of ashes, imprisoned in a cramped urn, unable to communicate with the outside world, utterly helpless. In vain his consciousness sought to remobilize its scattered energy, to pull itself together long enough to let out a shout, or better yet to make a fist and shatter the wall of the vase. But a body of powder does not obey the injunctions of the will as readily as it once did; it slips into indolence, it's just fine where it is and as it is, rid of those bones, released from that cruciform posture, in want of nothing, all desire vanquished.

After the panic and the desperate struggles, facing up to the facts, Crab's consciousness relaxed. After all, had it not always longed to free itself of the body? Pure consciousness, hovering above a little pile of ashes that never stirs — or that stirs only in order to collapse a little further, according to its whim — as alien to those ashes as heaven to earth, unimpeded, unhindered, as free and light as the day before the first day.

But a sentimental heir had the unfortunate idea of scattering the contents of the urn to the winds, and, after a brief ceremony conducted by unwelcome friends, Crab was returned to his native earth. He will soon be on his feet again.

51 Crab has been old for one minute, and the seconds are ticking by. A very old man. His heart is graying at the temples. Mirrors reflect his image in black and white, already yellowing.

Crab will lie low at home from now on, now that he has finally finished his memoirs. Does nothing. Never moves. Lips sealed. Eyes closed. Has an absent air about him. Nothing must ever happen to him again. Never again. The least little event would spoil everything. Even death. It's all in the book lying before him, his life in its entirety. Nothing to add. Finished.

But a fly lands on his cheek, and it's too much to bear.

At the end of the performance, the curtain did not fall—stuck in the flies no doubt—and since the audience expected the show to go on, Crab had no choice but to keep it up. He hesitated a moment; they thought he'd forgotten his lines, and the indulgent crowd gave him an ovation. Crab bowed and resolved to perform the whole play again from the beginning. There were a few catcalls at first, of course, but the more enlightened members of the crowd understood that this was a daring metaphor for the eternal return, or even a fierce satire of our serial existences, and urged silence upon the carping dullards. The second performance was applauded far more warmly than the first. But still the curtain did not fall.

With the third performance, the ranks of the carping dullards swelled considerably, while there was a sizable decrease in the number of supporters of a theater finally freed of the old conventions of dramaturgy. Crab was wise enough to stop there.

He improvised. He recited poems, and then the most famous harangues of the classical repertoire as they came to him, stuck together catch-as-catch-can, amalgamated, sometimes brutally juxtaposed; and Crab regularly exhumed the skull of Yorick from the pile of perfumed wigs—an old acquaintance, always a safe bet. A few offended spectators ostentatiously left the theater, but, on the whole, this comic indictment of the cultural sacred cows—to quote the explanation that a gentleman in the first row slid with his tongue into a perplexed little ear adorned with a diamond stud, and then repeated to the nude shrugging shoulder—was much appreciated: thunderous applause shook the rafters, but still the curtain did not fall.

Crab sang, danced, tossed off jump-rope rhymes, prayers, listed the major world capitals, the largest rivers, he spread his knowledge wide and thin, he counted as high as humanly possible, he explored the great moral and philosophical questions, he spun many a tale, he told the story of his life beginning with Darwin's childhood, he dissected his principal organs.... But still the curtain did not fall.

And then Crab sank into silence, slowly, inexorably, vertically, he sank in and eventually disappeared from the gaze of the audience. There was some confusion among the spectators, a moment of uncertainty, of incomprehension, but they quickly settled on the only credible hypothesis: a trapdoor had opened beneath Crab's feet—of course, there was a trapdoor concealed in the stage—and, by common agreement, this symbolic burial of the character, replacing the fall of the curtain or the sudden blackout that traditionally signifies the end of a show, was in itself worth the price of admission; with one blow it erased the long days of boredom that had preceded it. (*Applause.*)